THORNBERRY
MANOR

THE EMERALD

ANNE K. HAWKINSON

annehawkinson@outlook.com
www.annehawkinson.com

First Printing: January 2025
ISBN: 978-1-7320175-6-6
Cover design by Damonza

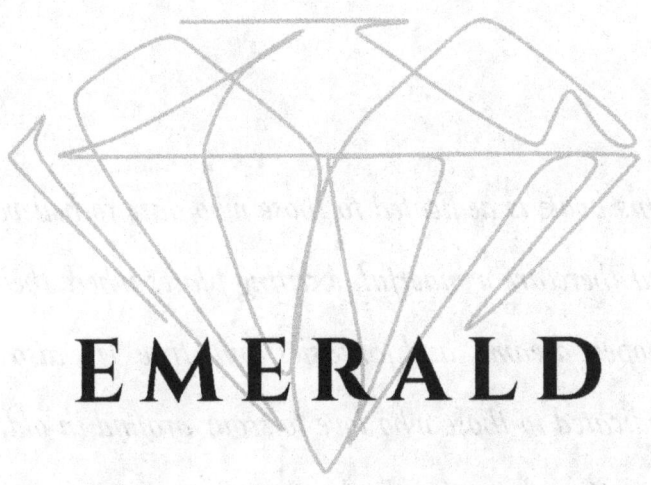

EMERALD

Some people believe wearing emeralds as talismans will

bring them riches, power, and eloquence along with an

improved memory and a sharpened wit.

Perhaps its most valuable power is bestowing the

ability to predict future events.

This book is dedicated to those who dare to believe that there are wonderful, exciting places where their hopes, dreams, and fantasies come true. It's also dedicated to those who love to scour around in old, forgotten places, for that's where priceless treasures and memories reside, waiting to be found. Last, but not least, to the steady supply of chocolate that got me to the last page.

ACKNOWLEDGEMENTS

Karen Feldman, English professor and editor extraordinaire, for her dedication and faith in my work, amazing attention to detail, and her invaluable notes and comments.

Barbara Prucha, for taking time from her busy life to spend it with my story. Her insight, plot catches, and suggestions are welcomed and much appreciated!

Karey Anne Gritz, for her calm confidence and unending encouragement, support, and computer wizardry. Because of her, my stories make the amazing transformation from dream to reality.

Finally, the necklace that inspired this story. An impulse purchase years ago (with a story of its own), it waited patiently until I discovered the amazing role it was destined to play.

TABLE OF CONTENTS

1

Chapter One

Paisley Venne huffed through the red, woolen scarf covering her nose and mouth, her useless brolly and parcel of worthless wedding invitations tucked under her arm. As she confronted the driving rain and gale force winds blustering in from the English Channel, a cluster of fishing boats lurched and listed perilously as they hugged the crescent-shaped cove past Luccombe Village, racing for the safety of Bembridge Harbour.

She whispered a prayer for them as she sprinted down the rain-slicked street and turned the corner where a long row of shops banded together, joining forces against the salty squall. The brass bell above the door jangled as she opened the door of Page-Turner Books and secured it behind her. There would be no customers until the storm passed, but she lowered the shade behind the *Closed* sign just the same. Most days she loved living in Bonchurch, but today wasn't one of them—first the weather, then the physical, painful reminder of the wedding that would never happen. *Better to find out now; the hurt and pain would only be worse later on.*

"That you, Paisley?" Molly, her mum, emerged from the back room carrying a stack of books, her careworn face softening to a smile now that her daughter was home safe. "I was getting worried about you. This storm…"

"I know, Mum. It'll pass, like they always do." Paisley opened her damp brolly and set it near the door, then tucked the parcel of invitations inside her coat. She wasn't in the mood for another wedding cancellation discussion even though her mum agreed with her.

Paisley knew she'd done the right thing after confronting Noah and a woman she'd never seen before cozied up in the corner of the local pub. He'd been dragging his feet every time she pressed him to partake in planning the wedding; now she knew why. The red flags had been flapping right in front of her face, but she hadn't been paying attention. Perhaps she'd been ignoring them, hoping they'd go away. Paisley pushed the painful memories away and inhaled the scent of seasoned, aged wood, leather-bound books, and the scented candles, sachets, and oils for sale in the shop.

"I thought I'd do some cleaning and put out the stock that came yesterday as long as the shop is closed. Want to give me a hand?" Molly brushed her hands on her apron, then tightened the scarf around her curly, dark hair streaked with silver strands. Her amber eyes warmed and relaxed now that Paisley was home.

"Sure. Let me change real quick, and I'll be right back." Paisley gave her mum a kiss and quick hug. "You worry too much."

"I know. But you're my girl."

"Your favorite and only girl," Paisley reminded her with a laugh. "And your grown-up girl." The wooden planked floors under the rug creaked in their predictable places as Paisley walked to the back of the store and trotted up the stairs to the converted flat where they lived.

It was small but comfortable and cosy. After all, it was only the two of them now. Each of their small bedrooms faced the waterfront with a sitting room in between. On the other side of the short hall, the kitchen, bathroom, and a small storage room filled the remaining space. It was convenient, living above the shop, but the size of their lodgings was a subtle, constant reminder to prioritize what one actually needed with available space at a premium. She threw the parcel of invitations on her bed, wondering how best to dispose of them; they'd never be addressed, posted, or gleefully plucked from a recipient's post box. Setting a match to them would be a fitting way to put it all behind her, but she didn't want to destroy the shop and their home in the process. Perhaps when the storm passed, she would use the base of the small barbeque grill in the back yard.

The compact, walled-in garden was a pleasant space, sheltered from the salt and wind by the two-story buildings hugging the coast. Solidly protected, it thrived with its tidy rows of vegetables, pots of flowers and herbs, and a comfortable, wooden bench weathered grey by the sun, wind, and rain. As Paisley grabbed a fizzy pop from the refrigerator, she glanced out the back window, hoping the staked tomatoes and beans would be safe from the current onslaught. So far, the last of the season were holding their own. Her mum had already taken the hanging pots down; they'd get the benefit of the rain without the danger of being buffeted by the wind and crashing to the ground.

"Those two boxes need to go on the 19th Century Female Authors table," her mum explained as she unrolled the promotional posters that would hang above.

4

"They were so talented," Paisley answered. "Wouldn't it be something if they could know how successful and popular their books were today?" She added copies of Jane Austen's *Pride and Prejudice* and Mary Shelley's *Frankenstein* to the stacks of books by Emily, Anne, and Charlotte Brontë. "Maybe we need another table; there are more women that aren't as well known or celebrated, and we should include them if we can."

"See what we've got on the shelves; we can slide two tables together and expand our display. I can always put in a rush order, depending on what you find and want to include."

Paisley found copies of *Cranford* and *Wives and Daughters* by Elizabeth Gaskell and *Lady Audley's Secret* and *Aurora Floyd* by Mary Elizabeth Braddon. "I feel better now," she said as she moved things around. "They deserve a place at the table, too. And I'll keep searching for more." She stepped back to critique the appearance of the display. "We're running the promotion for the rest of November and all of December, right?"

"Right." Molly ducked into the storeroom and returned with a step ladder. "Can you get these up for me? I'm not thrilled about climbing ladders these days."

Paisley climbed up and hung the posters from the ceiling hooks over the table; they rotated slowly when the air moved through the heating vents above the windows. "I'm gonna get you one of those extension arms with the hook on the end in case I'm not here when you want to take them down or change the others. Maybe one of those grabber things, too."

"Probably a good idea."

The aroma of vegetable soup in the slow cooker wafted down the stairs and floated amongst the titles and tables. "I'm glad I started dinner this morning. This time of day I sure don't want to think about cooking." Molly stacked the last cardboard box on top of the others near the stairs and turned back to Paisley. "Should we go up and eat now?"

"Sure, Mum. I'll just finish a couple bits here, and then we'll be good to go tomorrow—if the weather cooperates."

Molly dished up the thick, hearty soup and set a basket of rolls between them. After a few minutes of silence, she set down her spoon and studied Paisley spreading butter on her roll. "You picked them up—the invites, I mean."

"I did. Sally from Palmer's didn't charge me full cost for them. That was nice of her."

"Indeed." Another silence surrounded the small table. "I'm sorry about this whole business, Poppet."

"Don't be, Mum. I'm glad I found out about Noah before it was too late. I didn't make any other major wedding decisions, so I only invested time in planning something that isn't going to happen." She dipped her roll in the soup and took a bite. "I learned a valuable lesson—one I won't forget anytime soon."

Molly reached out and took Paisley's hands in hers. "Don't let this business with Noah sour you on love, Paisley. The man you're meant to be with is out there. Give it a little time, okay?"

Paisley glanced out the back window; it gave her a few seconds to gather up her patience and not hurt her mother's feelings. "Sure, Mum. What other option do I have?" Tears stung her eyelids. "I'll be 32 soon."

"Oh, posh. Don't worry about your age. You might be surprised if you give yourself a chance." Molly rose from the table and cleared her place, then pointed at Paisley's. "Still working on yours?"

"No, I'm done. I'll cover it and have it for lunch tomorrow." Paisley put her dinner away and watched the news and a sitcom to keep her mum company, even though she wasn't really interested in either. At half-past nine, she kissed her mum goodnight. "Thanks for cooking. I'm going to turn in early; it's been kind of a hard day."

The storm was easing but still thrusting wind and rain at the shore and her window; perhaps by morning it would exhaust itself. She closed the drapes and turned her attention to the parcel of invitations she'd tossed on the bed. *Not yet.* After brushing her teeth and washing up, she crawled into bed and opened the padded, manila envelope and slid out the contents.

They were beautiful invitations, printed on the creamy-white paper with embossed blue, lavender, and pink forget-me-nots. Paisley had chosen them specifically for their symbolic meaning—remembrance, true love, and memories. The font was beautifully captured and carefully chosen; the deep, rich blue England Hand had a pretty, slanted script. It was all there—the names, wedding venue, and the date: Saturday, June 29th, 2024. The wedding that would never be.

She knew she'd made the right decision despite the tear that rolled down her cheek and dampened the pastel, floral bouquet.

2

Chapter Two

It turned out to be a good Saturday in the shop; the passing of a storm always boosted people's spirits and inspired them to venture out. The 19th century display was popular, and the volumes Paisley tied together with festive ribbon were plucked from the display as quickly as she could replenish them. A new supply of books to carry them through December was hastily ordered and would arrive Monday morning.

After an evening meal of takeaway fish and chips, Paisley curled up on the couch and flicked the TV remote while her mum sorted through the day's mail. "Oh my God," Molly blurted as she cast the pile aside that she'd already opened.

"What?" Paisley asked, her attention drawn to her mother's unexpected outburst. She picked up the envelope that had fluttered to the floor and read the return address.

Morgan and Butterfield
54 Bedford Row
London, UK EC1A

It looked like something from a solicitor. "Is it about Dad?" A respected judge, he had recently retired only to die after a freak slip and fall accident at a fishing pier up the shore. Paisley was secretly grateful it wasn't the one close to the shop; she didn't know how she could step out the door every day and be confronted with the place where her father died. Although the bulk of the paperwork surrounding his death had been dealt with, there continued to be the odd, straggling bit of business to address.

A slip of sadness floated across her mother's eyes but dissipated quickly as she shook her head and lifted her hand, gesturing for Paisley to be quiet and listen. Molly cleared her throat and prepared to share the contents of the letter. "It's completely unexpected, but exciting. You'll see."

She took a deep breath, put a hand to her chest, and began to read.

Paisley sat in stunned silence as her mind tried to wrap itself around the words her mother read from the letter. When she finished, Paisley reached for it and whispered, "Can I see it?"

"Of course," her mother answered. "Do you think it's real, or some sort of scam?"

"I'm not sure." She looked at the phone number listed on the letterhead. "It's Saturday, and they're probably closed, but I can leave a message." Paisley pulled her phone out of her purse and took a photo of the letter. "Let's give it a shot."

She dialed the number, waited, and mouthed the word *voicemail*. Holding the letter in front of her, she left a message. "Hello. My name is Paisley Venne, and I'm calling on behalf of my mother, Molly Hicks Venne, about a letter she received from your office regarding a property transfer. I'll call again on Monday. Thank you."

Paisley hung up and typed the name of the law firm in the Internet search box on her phone. "Let's see if they have a website and what it looks like." She typed the name Morgan and Butterfield, added the word London, and tapped the blue Go button. "Well, they look legit, and their contact information matches what is in this letter, so let's see

11

what happens when I call on Monday." Paisley set her phone aside and focused on the letter. "If this is authentic, it sounds like you're about to inherit a piece of property in Hertfordshire. Did you know that anything like this was in your family?"

Her mother shook her head, her eyes sparkling with the possibility. "I had no idea. I mean, I'm English, but I never had much interaction with my distant relatives. People talk about their ethnicity and all, but it never really goes any further than that." She tapped her chin with her index finger as an idea formulated, then grabbed Paisley's hand. "You know what? I'm going to get a subscription to one of those genealogy sites. I've been wanting to do it for a long time, and this is the perfect excuse to find out more about my ancestors."

"Are you sure you don't want to wait until we hear back?"

"Not really. Regardless of what happens with them, I still want to do some research. It'll be fun." Paisley loved the sound of her mum's laughter. Since her father's passing, it had become something of a rarity, and it warmed her heart to hear sounds of joy and happiness again.

Paisley handed the letter to her mother and reluctantly pushed aside a myriad of curious, swirling thoughts. "Let's see what's on the telly, okay?"

Three hours later, she curled up in bed with her laptop and searched the Internet for Thornberry Manor. The image that popped up was blurry; Paisley leaned into the monitor and gasped at the stately, stone manor house. It wasn't a recent photo, judging by the appearance of the grounds and gardens. They appeared to be suffering from overgrowth and neglect, but Paisley was drawn to the beauty she hoped was merely waiting to be revealed. Were those climbing roses clinging to the stone? She couldn't wait to share the photo with her mum.

Paisley squinted at the photo on the screen; it was hopelessly out of focus, but what she could make out of the blurred outline fascinated her. Stone steps curved alongside a ground-level foundation, a main story, and a generous second story with attic windows near a roof line that jutted out here and there. The exterior was grey stone, and the windows had diamond-shaped panes. A rounded hump at one end of the house looked like it was once a conservatory or greenhouse. What looked like a walled garden extended beyond the double doors on the two sides of the house Paisley could see. All of it was cloaked in a tangled mess of vegetation; ivy and what looked like more climbing roses clinging to spaces around the doors and windows, along the wall, and sprawling onto the grounds below. She couldn't wait to see it in person.

From an online map, it looked to be a short distance north of London and easily accessible by train. Once there, they could hire a car to get them the rest of the way. She was sure her mum would want to see it, and they could find someone to run the bookshop for a day or two while they were away. Their neighbor, Alice Clarke, had stepped in to help when her father died, and Paisley was sure she'd be willing to help them out again.

She pulled up the notes app on her phone and typed in reminders of what she'd ask Andrew Collins (the solicitor who'd written the letter) when she called back on Monday: 1) Electricity? Does it exist? Turn it on? 2) Plumbing status? Water? Hot/cold? Toilets/baths? 3) When was the last time someone lived there? 4) Grocery/supply store nearby?

When they visited, it would be helpful to know what to expect. The grounds looked neglected, and she had no interior photos. If gardens were not regularly tended to, they could curl and crawl their way out of control in no time. "Enough for today," she announced with a yawn as she stretched her arms to the ceiling.

Paisley laughed to herself as she set the phone down and turned on the bathtub faucet. She was getting ahead of herself, going off on a tangent. She did that sometimes. The property may not be worth salvaging or may need repairs that were beyond their financial means.

Still, ideas about restoring and transforming it poked and prodded at her. "One step at a time," she reminded herself as she slipped into the steamy, lavender-scented water.

3

Chapter Three

"It's the solicitor's office," Paisley whispered to her mum as she rang up a sale. "I'm gonna take it upstairs." Molly nodded but remained focused and smiling at the young couple she was helping.

"Yes, hello. This is Paisley Venne. I left a message over the weekend about a letter my mother received regarding a property in Hertfordshire. Can you connect me to someone I can discuss it with?"

"Hello, Ms. Venne. My name is Nancy, and I'll transfer you to Andrew Collins."

"Thank you." She sat on the couch and pulled up the photo she'd taken of the letter, scanning it quickly as she waited to be connected.

"Ms. Venne?"

"Yes."

"Hello. I'm Andrew Collins, the solicitor who drafted and sent the letter to your mother."

"Hello. Nice to meet you, sort of. So, what can you tell me about Thornberry Manor and how it's come to her?"

"Well, the last, living relative was a man by the name of John B. Hicks. He was your grandfather Richard Hicks' first cousin. Died in September of 2023. His wife Margaret predeceased him, and their only daughter Rachel passed in 1991. There are no other living relatives between John and Molly, your mother, so the property passes to her."

"So, what happens now? Where do we go from here?"

"Well, there's paperwork that needs to be drawn up. And a valuation needs to be made; that will determine if there is any inheritance tax that will be due."

"Maybe my next step is to travel there with my mum and meet with an appraiser, then?"

"That might be a good place to start. If there is any tax due, it needs to be paid by the end of the sixth month after the current owner has passed. Since John passed in

September, you have until March of next year to pay any taxes that might be due."

Paisley froze at the thought of hundreds or thousands of pounds of inheritance tax. Where would they come up with that much money? Andrew seemed to sense her concern and added, "Of course, if the property is valued at less than £325,000 no taxes will be due." She sighed louder than she intended and was sure he'd heard her. "Let's take it one step at a time. Travel there with your mum as soon as you can and meet with an appraiser. Then we'll go from there."

He was right. Don't think too far down the road. One step at a time. "Thank you, Mr. Collins. I'll need to find an appraiser nearby who can meet us there."

"I can recommend someone from the area that we work with. His name is Charles Childress. If you want to give me your email address, I'll send his contact information to you, and you can proceed from there."

Paisley spelled it out as she stood and stared out the window at the calm, undulating water. "We'll need to gain access to the house. Do you know who has the keys?"

"I will find out and see that Mr. Childress has them when he meets with you."

"Thank you, Mr. Collins. You've been very helpful. I will contact you along the way as we move through this process."

"Very good. Have a pleasant day, Ms. Venne."

"Goodbye, Mr. Collins." After Paisley hung up, she made a mental note to research lodging accommodations and transportation once she talked to her mum about the best time to travel to Thornberry Manor. She wanted to go right away—today.

"Paisley, while you're up there, how about making us some lunch? There are fixings for sandwiches in the fridge."

"Sure, Mum. I'm on it."

* * *

With the shop closed and supper dishes drying in the rack, Paisley sat with Molly on the couch in the sitting room with her laptop and penciled notes. "So, here's what we can do. We'll take a taxi to the ferry, then the train to Keighley Station. That's going to take most of the day, so I found a few places where we can stay in Keighley. The next day we can hire a car to take us to Thornberry.

"I'm going to contact this Charles Childress and make sure he can meet us there with the keys, and I have a list of questions started about the property. Like is the electricity still working? If so, can it be turned on while we're there? What about water and plumbing? I think we need to know what we're dealing with before we make any decisions about it. What do you think?"

Molly leaned over, elbow on her knee and chin in hand as she peered at the notes. Paisley forced herself to be patient and silent; she'd been working on the ideas swirling in her head since she'd talked to Mr. Collins, and her mum was seeing them for the first time. "I suppose that will work," she answered, leaning back against the couch. "But who will watch the shop while we're away? We can't close at such a busy time."

"I bet Alice will be willing to help us out for a few days. If we go in the middle of the week, it won't be as busy. She did a great job when we had to be gone for Dad's funeral." Molly nodded but said nothing. "Can you give her a call and see if she'd be willing to help us out for a few days? If she's up for it, I can contact some of the inns in Keighley and arrange rooms and transportation." Paisley nudged her mum. "Yeah. Call her now."

As Molly looked around for her phone, Paisley offered up a suggestion. "You don't have to tell her where we're going or what we're doing if you don't want to. Not yet. We don't really know much ourselves at this point. Maybe just tell her we need to be away from the shop for a few days and ask if she can help us out. Tell her it will be the middle of the week, and see if there are any dates she's not available. Once we know that, I can get reservations made and our transport finalized."

Molly opened the contact list on her phone and tapped Alice's number. "I'm sure she'll help us out." She winked at Paisley as the phone rang. "Hello, Alice? It's Molly Venne."

4

Chapter Four

Despite the exhaustion from the taxi, ferry, and train ride to Keighley, Paisley tossed and turned all night. It wasn't just the unfamiliar room, bed, and sounds on the street outside; it was the thought of seeing Thornberry Manor for the first time. The estate that now belonged to her mother, snoring softly in the bed next to hers.

She'd researched and printed out what little information she could find along with what Mr. Collins had sent her; perhaps the local church or historical society would have something more. They wouldn't have time to visit on this trip, but she could ask if the opportunity arose and put it on a future list if they decided to keep the property.

What she'd been able to find was assembled in a binder with coloured divider tabs and blank, lined paper for notes in each section. Everything they discovered would be kept in one place—interior, exterior, utilities, grounds, history, and a few, blank extras she knew would present themselves once they arrived and started inspecting and exploring. The legal paperwork was at home in a separate binder; Paisley didn't want the weighty numbers and legal jargon burying the excitement that was building inside of her. A manor house! Gardens! Extensive grounds and a small lake! It sounded like a dream come true, whatever its condition might be. She gently pushed the visions of Pemberley from the film version of *Pride and Prejudice* from her imagination. It couldn't possibly be as grand or in the same, pristine condition. But it might be grand enough.

Molly stirred as Paisley checked the time on her phone. She could be in and out of the bathroom before her mum woke, and they'd be that much closer to breakfast, boxed lunches, and meeting Finlay, their driver. It was a happy coincidence that he was an employee at the Silent Inn; he would drop them off in the morning, run his other errands, and pick them up in the afternoon for the return trip to the inn. Paisley wished they had more than one day at

Thornberry, but reminded herself to take things one step at a time.

She leaned down and smiled at her mum who stretched, rubbed her eyes, and looked at Paisley with sudden alarm. "What time is it? Did I sleep too long?"

"No, you're fine, Mum. I'm going downstairs to check on our box lunches and make sure Finlay is around and ready to take us to Thornberry. Come down as soon as you're ready. We'll have breakfast and be on our way."

Molly whipped the covers off, slid out of bed, and gathered up her clothes. "I'll be down as soon as I can. I can't wait to see the place."

Olivia was putting out a fresh plate of scones when Paisley approached her. "Good morning, Olivia." Her stomach rumbled as she tried to discreetly inhale the aromas wafting around them. "Everything smells delicious." She observed Olivia quickly, wondering how she could stay so trim and fit while surrounded by food day in and day out. Her red, curly hair was tied back, and she wore a deep, green apron that matched the color of her eyes.

"Morning, Paisley. Thanks. Did you and your mum sleep well?"

"We did, thanks. She'll be down in a bit for breakfast, then Finlay will take us to Thornberry." She looked around the dining room, but didn't see him among the guests. "Is he around?"

"To be sure. He's having his breakfast just now, then he'll fill the car with petrol and be ready when you are." Olivia gestured toward the kitchen. "I have your lunches in the kitchen. Let me know when you're ready to leave and I'll collect them for you."

"I will. Thank you so much." She knew Olivia was busy but couldn't help asking. "Do you know much about Thornberry and the people who lived there?"

"The Hicks family, you mean?"

Paisley nodded eagerly. "Yes!"

Olivia shook her head as she scanned the dining room. "My grandfather may have known some who would have been his contemporaries, but he passed years ago. My suggestion is the registry office on Church Road. They may have some documents on file relating to the family."

"Thank you, Olivia. I'll remember that." She turned in time to see her mum enter the dining room and walk toward them. "I'm glad she showed up. I was about to start without her."

Olivia laughed, greeted Molly, and turned back to the kitchen. "I'll let you get to it, then."

Breakfast was delicious and buffet-style, with a generous selection of traditional English breakfast offerings along with porridge, eggs, toast, and pastries. Paisley tried to pace herself, but two things hindered her in that respect. One, everything was *so* good, and two, she was anxious for them to be on their way.

They met Lewis, Olivia's husband, when they saw Finlay pull up with the car. Tall and willowy with hints of grey in his hair and beard, he had a warm, generous smile that reminded Paisley of her father. "All set with your lunches, I see." He grinned with a wink and opened the back door of the car for them. "Give Finlay a call when you're ready to get picked up; he'll let you know how much lead time he needs."

"Thank you, Lewis. My mother and I really appreciate your arranging transport for us."

"We're happy to help out if and when we can. On your way, then, and good luck at Thornberry."

The December sun was as pale as a worn-out highlighter and provided little warmth, but Paisley appreciated the dancing shadows it created along the tree-lined roadway. Their wool coats would keep them warm if there was no heat in the house or there was time to wander the grounds. "How far is it from the inn?" she asked tall, handsome Finlay.

He glanced over at her with kind, blue eyes. "Not far, really. Thirty minutes or so, depending on the weather and roads."

They kept up the friendly, general banter until an alert on Paisley's phone brought a hush to the interior of the car and its occupants. "Good morning, Mr. Childress. Yes, we're on our way. About ten minutes or so?" Finlay's head nodded in agreement with Paisley's estimation. "Great. See you then. 'Bye."

Finlay looked at Paisley, then into the rear-view mirror at Molly. "So, not really my business, but if you don't mind my asking, what's sending you to Thornberry Manor? There's no one living there now since John Hicks died in September. Are you looking to buy the place?"

"Not really."

"I know it needs work and looking after. I'm pretty handy, and I know a group of guys who can tackle most of what the place needs. Besides working for Olivia and Lewis, I have my own business doing construction and maintenance."

Finlay stopped the car in front of a large set of ironwork gates anchored in stone pillars. A companion arch spanned the drive with graceful, powerful intertwining letters *T* and *M*—Thornberry Manor. They'd finally arrived.

Finlay jumped out and opened the gates, pushing them into the tall, overgrown grass along the drive. Molly rolled down her window, and Paisley leaned forward, straining for a glimpse of the main house. The birch and beech trees had lost their leaves, but the pines and cypress obscured the view, as if she were being blindfolded prior to receiving a long-awaited surprise.

Paisley was anxious and reluctant at the same time. She wanted to savor every moment of her first visit to Thornberry Manor. "Slow, Finlay. Go slow, please." Paisley rolled down her window and deeply inhaled the thick aroma of pine and winter-wet leaves. "It's so beautiful here."

"Indeed. It's lovely," Molly added. "So different from Bonchurch and the sea."

With a slight curve to the left, the main house came into view. "Oh, my God," Paisley whispered as she grabbed Finlay's sleeve. "Please stop, Finlay. I need to get out and see it from here."

5

Chapter Five

The blurred photo she'd received from Andrew Collins came into clear focus. Thornberry Manor stood proudly in the distance, firmly nestled against a backdrop of trees with a small, shimmering lake at its feet. Paisley imagined herself in a horse-drawn carriage, passing the eastern shore of the lake and coming to a stop in front of the entrance. "Okay, we can go now," she whispered to Finlay, as if speaking in a normal tone would break the spell. It wasn't Pemberley, but it was theirs, she hoped.

As they pulled up, they agreed on a time for Finlay's

return to bring them back to the inn. "Your man isn't here yet. Do you want me to wait?"

"No, we're fine, Finlay. We can explore some of the grounds while we wait. I'm sure Mr. Childress will be here soon."

Finlay reached into the car and handed Paisley their boxed lunches and Paisley's binder. "You don't want to forget these and have them riding around with me all day." His blue eyes warmed when their hands touched during the exchange. Paisley blushed and quickly changed the subject.

"You said you're a handyman, right?" Finlay nodded. "Well," Paisley continued, "if things go well, would you be willing to come and inspect the house and tell us what needs to be done to set it to rights?"

"I'd be happy to." He reached into his shirt pocket and handed her his card. "Has my email and phone number. Let me know when you're ready and what you need. I can meet you here, or we can ride together if you're staying at the inn."

"Thank you, Finlay. For now, keep your fingers crossed that everything works out."

"I'll do that, Ms. Venne. Whatever *everything* is."

"Paisley. Please call me Paisley."

"All right. Enjoy exploring Thornberry, Paisley, and I'll see you back here at four."

"Thanks, Finlay. See you then."

"Thank you, Finlay," Molly said, approaching them with a matchmaker's smile that she shared equally with both of them. "I can't wait to see what Thornberry has in store for us."

"Enjoy your day, ladies."

With Finlay gone, Paisley turned to face Thornberry. "Oh, Mum, it's real, and it's yours! Can you believe it?"

"Well, it's starting to sink in now that we're actually here."

Paisley ran up one side of a matching pair of curved, stone steps leading to the entrance. The weathered, double doors of oak were massive, sturdy, and securely fastened. "Locked," Paisley announced as she tapped the iron door knocker. As she descended the other set of steps, she waved at Molly to join her. "Let's have a look around at the outside while we wait for Mr. Childress."

"I'll leave our lunches and your binder here on the wall so Mr. Childress knows we've arrived and are here somewhere."

After admiring the grey, stone facade and speculating about what rooms were behind certain windows, they moved to the west side of the house to what Paisley had guessed from the photo was a walled garden and the remains of a conservatory or greenhouse. "Oh, look, Mum! Isn't it beautiful?"

"Well, it probably was at some point, but it's fallen into disrepair." *She's right*, Paisley thought, but refused to give up on the possibilities that still remained. Part of the conservatory roof had fallen in, and the glass panes overhead that remained looked to be in danger of coming down with the next strong gust of wind. The basic framework was intact, but exposure to the elements had become an invitation for nature to step in and begin reclaiming it as her own.

"Let's not give up on it, Mum. There's still so much to see. Finlay's a handyman who knows other craftsmen, and he's offered to help us out." She walked over and gently touched the thorny branches of the climbing roses. "These old roses just need pruning and some fertilizer and they'll be happy again. Don't you wonder how old they are and who planted them? I wish they could talk; I wager they'd have some amazing stories to tell." She walked around the interior of the conservatory, pointing out what she recognized. "You love to garden, Mum. Wouldn't you love to have a go at this with your pruners and shovel?"

"I would, but I'm not getting any younger, and there's the shop to tend to."

"Promise you'll keep an open mind, Mum, and not let it overwhelm you."

Molly looked around, trying to smile despite the surroundings. "I'll try. Really, I will."

The sound of car tires crunching on the gravel drive postponed any further discussion of repair and refurbishment for the moment. "I hope it's Mr. Childress," Molly said as they left the conservatory.

After gently wrestling the fragile door closed, Paisley glanced beyond the conservatory and noticed parts of a flagstone walkway, now overgrown, leading to what looked like a cemetery. There was a low, stone wall and an iron entrance gate that sagged into the ground, probably due to one of the hinges giving way. In shades of grey, the stones huddled together, some leaning as if they'd grown weary of their duty while others remained stoically upright. "I need to check that out," she said to herself. "Mum, there's a cemetery here." But her mother was out of earshot, and Paisley's words were gathered up for safekeeping by the brisk, December breeze.

6

Chapter Six

Molly was already shaking hands with the sturdy Charles Childress when Paisley joined them. He looked to be about her mum's age with salt-and-pepper hair, beard, and moustache. His solid physique was well-settled in a suit and overcoat that looked a bit out of place in the unkept, slightly bedraggled setting of Thornberry Manor.

He smiled as he extended his hand to Paisley. "Charles Childress. It's a pleasure to meet you and your mother."

"Nice to meet you, Mr. Childress. Thank you for

taking the time to help us out."

"Andrew and I are childhood friends as well as business colleagues, so I'm happy to give him a hand." He looked up at the front facade with a sigh. "She looks a bit tired and worn, but she's beautiful just the same. Let's take a look inside."

Molly scooped up their lunch boxes and Paisley her binder as Mr. Childress led the way up the stairs, unlocked the door, and held it for them to enter ahead of him. Paisley gasped, her hand splayed on her chest as she stepped into the vestibule. It was bigger than her bedroom in Bonchurch with what looked like a slate floor and richly paneled walls. Straight ahead was a grand staircase covered in a dusty, crimson carpet, its balustrade a glorious curving of wood that paused at a generous, windowed landing before continuing to the first floor.

"Let's start on the ground floor and work our way upstairs," Charles suggested. A doorway to the right led to what looked like a study. Paisley glanced at the shelves of books, desk, and seating before following her mum and Charles in the opposite direction. "I suppose this would be the drawing room," he said.

Molly inspected the imposing fireplace, her hand gently sliding along the smooth mantle as silent, charred logs rested as if waiting to be re-ignited on its wide, iron grate.

"When was someone here last?" she asked. "I mean, actually living here."

Charles flipped open the folder he'd brought in with him. "Well, John lived here until he was admitted to hospital in September. So, the property has been unoccupied for a few months, but it appears as though some of the rooms may have been untouched, left as they were by those who were here before him. I visited after I was contacted by Andrew and took a quick walk through in preparation for our meeting today." He flipped through, then closed his folder. "I'd have to look at the residential records to see how long he actually lived here."

"I guess it doesn't really matter, at least as far as today's visit is concerned." Paisley opened her binder to the *Interior* tab, titled the page *Drawing Room*, and noted the fireplace, rugs, and furnishings. "I'm going to take photos of each room so I don't forget anything—I'll be behind you as you move from room to room." She was grateful to see a water closet in a small room off the hall and reminded herself to ask Mr. Childress about the utilities and water before their visit ended.

Large doors with glass panels led from the drawing room down several steps to the conservatory Paisley and her mum had explored while they were waiting for Mr. Childress to arrive. They hadn't gotten far enough to discover the wrought-iron table and chairs arranged to enjoy the view of what was probably once a beautiful orange tree. A few dried, dusky oranges clung to its branches as if to signal to anyone looking at it that it was still alive. *Spare me. Help me* it seemed to say. Paisley gently plucked the dull, wrinkled fruit from the tree, inhaled their faint hint of citrus, and set them on the table next to the tree. After taking a photo, she reassured it in her thoughts. *Hang on. Help is coming.*

They returned across the vestibule and entered the study; Paisley made sure to photograph the curved alcove seating area with generous floor-to-ceiling windows. "What a perfect place to read or just be alone with your thoughts," she mused aloud.

"Indeed," Mr. Childress said as he pointed to another fireplace, a bit smaller than the one in the drawing room but perfectly proportioned to the size of the room.

Paisley was anxious to see the upstairs, but they passed the grand staircase once again and entered the dining room on the same side of the house as the study. "Oh my!" Molly exclaimed. "Another fireplace, and look at this magnificent table and chairs; it looks like mahogany." She walked along the backs of the chairs, counting as she went. "Seven on each side, plus one at the foot and head. That would be quite a gathering. And look, another alcove similar to the one in the study."

Paisley was busy scribbling notes and taking photos of each room; she wished she had more time to explore every detail, but today would not be that day. She'd never been inside the beautiful manor house, but she felt like it was welcoming her and that she belonged there; like it was home—her family's home. Somehow, someway, she'd find a way to keep it from being sold.

A wooden bench, upholstered in shades of claret and gold sat under the windows of the stairway landing and overlooked the back of the property. The leafless deciduous and protective, blue-green conifers had been planted in a careful arrangement to make them look as random as possible. Beyond the planned parkland was the forest, planted in nature's blueprint. Another stairway with about half the steps of the first led them to the first floor.

Paisley stopped at the top of the landing and saw how cleverly it diverted into three, separate directions leading to three bedrooms and another water closet tucked into a discreet, closet-sized space. They all had fireplaces that were extensions of the ones in the rooms on the ground floor below them.

The first one they visited had windows that faced west and overlooked the roof of the conservatory. What might have been a beautifully furnished room had become a storage cache full of boxes, random furnishings reminiscent of the past, and more contemporary items like a space heater, suitcase with wheels, and an elongated box full of tubes of holiday wrapping paper. It looked like a combination antique store and modern-day storage locker.

The second bedroom must have been John's and overlooked the main entrance, the curving drive, and the lake. The antique bed was covered in a present-day blue and grey stripe, and a small bureau and night table were on either side. Paisley suddenly felt like an intruder in this room and silently apologized to John for their presence and inspection of what must have been his personal things. She took a few notes and a photo but was anxious to leave.

The east-facing bedroom seemed to welcome her with open arms. Paisley immediately relaxed as she passed the fireplace and looked out the windows that would catch the morning sun. This room was definitely used by a female with its soft florals and ruffled shams on the canopy bed, and it had an added feature the others didn't in the form of a separate bath and dressing room. *Was this room used by a relative of John's?* She walked around the room, taking photos and jotting down notes as fast as she could. "This would be my room after a makeover," she said to herself after her mum and Charles had moved on.

"Where's the kitchen?" Molly asked from somewhere down the hall.

"Oh, on the lower level. There's access from the outside—did you notice the small staircase next to the conservatory? The inside access is past the staircase on the ground level. We can go there now if you like."

"Oh, yes. I'd like to see the kitchen." Molly stopped and looked over her shoulder as they descended the stairs. "C'mon, Paisley. We're going to the kitchen."

It was huge, with some original features intact, like the cavernous mouth of a cooking fireplace, the smooth flagstone floor, and hatch-marked work tables. Shafts of light from the windows high on the walls pierced bits and pieces of the shadowed interior. Paisley was relieved to see that the kitchen was somewhat modernized with a stove, oven, and sinks with running water. "What about the electric?" Paisley flicked a light switch on. "I see that it works, but is it up to code? Is that something we'd need inspected?"

"Yes," Charles answered as he jotted down a few, quick notes. "That would be the next step whether you decide to keep the property or sell—an inspection and appraisal." He looked at his watch and closed his folder. "I have to leave for another appointment—you have transportation back to where you're staying?"

"We do, thanks," Molly answered as she closed the oven door.

Charles reached into his pocket and handed a set of keys to Molly. "I took the liberty of making a set for you. That way, you can come and go as you need to, and you won't have to wait around for someone to let you in."

"That was quite considerate. Thank you."

"You're most welcome." He reached out and shook hands with Paisley. "It was a pleasure meeting you. Please feel free to call with any questions or concerns you may have. I'm sure there will be some."

After Molly shook his hand, she gestured toward the stairs. "I'll see you out and grab our lunches. I think I left them in the vestibule."

"We can go out through the servant's entrance. I didn't get a chance to show that to you."

"Brilliant." Molly turned back to Paisley as she followed Charles to the darkened stairway in the back corner of the kitchen. "I'll be right back."

Paisley tried the faucet and was relieved to see clear, cold water fill the bottom of the sink. She dug through the cupboards, discovered a large, metal pitcher, and listened to the splashing against its sides as it filled with water. *Who held this pitcher and filled it before me?* Hurrying up the stairs, she found her way past the vestibule to the conservatory where the thirsty orange tree waited for her. After gathering up the dry, brittle leaves, she roughed up the soil with her fingers and gently emptied the pitcher around its base. "It's not much, but it'll keep you alive until I can come back and take care of you. Besides, December is a good time for you to rest."

Paisley met her mum as she passed the vestibule. "Where do you want to eat?"

"How about in the study? We can call Finlay now, and then look around some more while we wait." They each settled in a leather armchair and tucked into the sandwiches, fruit, and biscuits that Olivia had packed for them. "It feels alright in here. Even in December, the morning sun, pale as it is, did a good job of warming up the room."

It was gratifying to sit down and take it all in. Their chairs faced the quiet, dormant fireplace, there was a thick, well-made carpet under their feet that needed a good cleaning, and the room itself exuded a scent of old, polished wood and the subtle, historical wafting of old books waiting for their covers to be lifted once again.

Paisley absorbed it all while she waited for her mum to finish her lunch and close the lid on her takeaway box. She leaned forward in her chair, eyes bright with expectation. "Well, Mum, what do you think?"

7

Chapter Seven

The rhythmic, breaking waves at home in Bonchurch took some getting used to after the silent expanse of the slumbering Thornberry Manor. Paisley and her mum had touched on a few subjects concerning the property but hadn't had a serious discussion about it or come to a decision one way or the other.

With the shop closed and dinner over, Paisley decided it was time to broach the subject and find a way forward regarding the property. She handed her mum a fresh mug of tea and settled herself in the chair next to her. "So,

Mum. About Thornberry. I got an email from Andrew Collins today, and he's wanting us to schedule the inspection and appraisal. I think we need to have a serious discussion about it and make a decision."

Molly took a sip of her tea. "What's to decide? As beautiful as it is, we can't take on a property like Thornberry. What would we do with it? And it's so far away from here."

Paisley wriggled in her chair, eager to share the ideas that had been whirling around since Thornberry had come into their lives. "Okay, so hear me out before you say anything." She froze for a moment, unsure of where to start. "First of all, I'm hoping the inspection doesn't show too many problems; John was living there, so it must have been somewhat functional. Second, if the appraisal is under £325,000, we won't have to pay any inheritance tax. I'm hoping we can transform it into a sort of B&B—a place for vacations, retreats, and family gatherings. Things like that. It's in a beautiful part of the country; I'm sure tourists would want to spend time at a place as beautiful as Thornberry could be again."

"I understand your enthusiasm, but where are you going to get the money to restore it and get it ready for guests?" Molly took a gulp of her tea and waved her hand in front of her open mouth to ease the burning sensation. "Who would be there to oversee the day-to-day operation?"

"Well, I did some research, and there's an organization called Historic England that offers grants to cover some or all of the repairs of historic sites. We'd need to see if Thornberry Manor qualifies as a historic site. If not, I'd be willing to go to the banks and see what they could do to help, but I'd want to try the grant route first. I need to contact them right away, because their site says they can't cover any work that is done before receiving the grant."

"It sounds like you've already made up your mind about keeping it."

Paisley nearly jumped out of her chair. "Oh, Mum, we've got to try, don't you think? I could travel back and forth when I need to if you'd rather stay here and look after the shop. And I'm sure Alice will help us out if you want to come along. After Christmas, maybe we could even close for a few days; it's not that busy in January, anyway. I could go up after Christmas and start on some of the basic cleanup. That wouldn't cost much, and it would give us a good look at what needs to be done in what order."

Paisley reached out and took her mother's hands in hers. "It's yours, Mum. Thornberry Manor belongs to you, and I think we need to do all that we can to keep it in the family. Don't you agree?" She sat back, shaking her head. "I don't know what it is, but there's something about it that keeps tugging at me, telling me that it belongs to us and we belong to it. I think we owe it to ourselves, and to Thornberry, to try. Don't you?"

"You understand that it will be an awful lot of work, don't you?"

"I do, Mum, and I get overwhelmed thinking about it, too. But I keep thinking if we take it one step at a time, it will be easier to mentally and financially manage. I can do a lot of the general cleanup, and there's Finlay and his connections that can help us whether or not we get the grant."

Molly smiled, her eyes brightening with enthusiasm. "If you're sure…"

"I'm more than sure, Mum—I don't quite understand it myself, but I've never been more sure of anything in my life. How many people in the world find out that a manor house and grounds suddenly belong to them? If we can find a way for it to support itself, that's even better, don't you think?"

"You're right. It's worth a try."

Paisley jumped up from her chair, hugged her mum, and grabbed her phone. "I can't wait to get started! I'm going to contact Andrew to schedule the inspection and assessment. I can meet with them and do some cleanup while I'm there. I'll ask Finlay about how to dispose of trash and yard waste; he'll know all about that, I'm sure."

After pressing the send button on the emails to Andrew and Finlay, doubt and uncertainty crept in, threatening to smother the excitement she'd felt earlier. It was a Herculean task. What if she failed, and it all came to nothing? There was no guarantee she'd receive any grant money for repairs and restoration, and bringing Thornberry Manor up to standards would be a costly endeavor. What was the alternative? Give up and let it deteriorate further, until some other developer would come along and buy it for a song?

"No!" she whispered aloud from beneath the quilt tucked up around her ears. This was *her* family's property, *her* family's legacy. She would not give up without a fight. She could do this, and she had people in her corner who would be willing to help.

Her screen lit up with a message from Noah. He was sorry for what happened and could they try and make a go of it? "Are you serious?" she whispered, the sting long gone, and her focus above and beyond any kind of life she would have had with him. Without answering, she deleted the message and blocked him from her contacts. "I should have done that a long time ago. Well, better late than never."

She turned off her phone and spent her last waking moments organizing and prioritizing tasks in her mind as her memory guided her on another visit to each and every room of Thornberry Manor.

Chapter Eight

It was a good, busy Christmas season at Page-Turner Books. January was predictably quiet, and Molly was happy to remain behind with Alice's offer to help with the annual inventory.

Paisley was equally happy to make the trip to Thornberry on her own. It wasn't that she didn't want her mum along or enjoy her company, but she was laser-focused on the tasks she wanted to accomplish and didn't want any distractions—human or otherwise. Finlay would meet her at the train station and drive her to Thornberry; she'd stay there instead of at the Silent Inn. If she had heat, water, and electricity, she could function and get things done. An extra bag of ingredients for easy meals like soup and sandwiches would be enough for this trip. Her mum had packed more than enough and added crisps, biscuits, and chocolates along with fruit and cheese. An online order of cleaning and other supplies would hopefully be waiting on the doorstep when she arrived.

She had Monday to work, the inspector and appraiser would visit on Tuesday, then she'd have two more days before returning home on Friday. Finlay would return on Wednesday to review the inspector's report and help her with the plan moving forward. He was there as promised, handsome and smiling. "Hello, Paisley. Good trip?"

"Hi, Finlay. Good, but long. I'll get used to it."

"Are you sure you don't want to stay at the inn tonight? I mean, have you had a chance to clean a space to sleep at the manor?"

"It won't take but a few minutes, and I can get started on some serious cleaning and yardwork right away in the morning because I'll already be there." He stopped the car, rolled down the window, and pointed at a fence line running along the road and across a field, over a hill, and out of sight. "This land belongs to the manor as well. It's rented out to the neighboring farmers who graze their sheep or grow grasses and grains. It's probably mentioned in the land abstract, but I wanted you to see where one of the property lines was."

"I had no idea. Thank you for showing me." Paisley immediately thought about a congenial working relationship with the farmers and welcoming whatever income the rent would bring to the manor's accounts. She made a mental note to start another list of questions for the appraiser and/or Andrew Collins.

The pale, January sun was clutching at the trees when Finlay opened the gates to Thornberry Manor. As she stepped out of the car into the brisk twilight, she prayed that the heat was on and working. Charles Childress had assured her that it would be.

Finlay looked at her with concern as he helped her with her bags. "You'll be okay here on your own?"

"I'll be fine as long as everything is on and functioning properly. If not, I'll deal with it tomorrow."

"You've already got a delivery." The packages were stacked next to the door, against the wall.

"Cleaning stuff and other supplies. Glamorous, huh?" she said with a laugh. "At any rate, I'm glad they arrived." He helped her carry them into the vestibule, then stopped before leaving.

"Call me old-fashioned, but I worry about you up

here all alone."

"I'll be fine, really."

"I don't live far from here, and you have my cell number, right?"

"I do. The appraiser and inspector will be here Tuesday, and you'll be here on Wednesday to help me with a plan. If something happens or I need help, I'll text or give you a call, okay?"

"Fair enough."

"Thank you, Finlay."

"You're welcome, Paisley." He took her hand and gave it a gentle squeeze. "Please be careful and don't take any unnecessary chances."

"I won't. Promise."

"I'll say good night then."

"Goodnight, Finlay. And thanks again. See you on Wednesday."

"Wednesday!" he called as he got into the car, waved to her, and pulled away.

It was a strange, unsettling feeling for a number of reasons. Paisley was used to being alone, but not in an isolated manor house that was still somewhat unfamiliar to her. There were no immediate neighbors on either side of her like at Bonchurch. This was her ancestral home, but she and Thornberry had just been introduced; it would take time for them to get to know each other.

It was warm enough in the house, but Paisley decided against sleeping in any of the bedrooms until she'd cleaned and organized them. She'd build a fire in the study and sleep there. It was cosy soon enough, and the books on the shelves would keep her company. Before she settled in, she needed to check one thing.

The conservatory was chilly, but not freezing. The orange tree was still standing, stark and stoic, branches outstretched but devoid of leaves. Paisley hoped it was merely dormant and not dead. *I'm here now. I will take care of you.* She found a bucket next to a potting table and filled it halfway. "Just a little for now, because you're supposed to be sleeping. I hope you're just sleeping." She watched the water slowly seep into the soil. "Tomorrow, I'll figure out a way to protect you from the cold. If I have to, I'll bring you inside. So, hang in there for tonight, and we'll come up with a game plan tomorrow."

Back in the study, she pulled the dusty drapes closed, and after a quick trip outside for dried leaves and kindling, managed to get a small fire burning. The chimney appeared to be clear and drafting properly once Paisley remembered to open the damper. Still, she'd keep it small until this chimney and the others could be inspected and cleaned properly. Perhaps tomorrow she'd sleep in one of the bedrooms. An idea popped into her head along with a promise to let her mum know she'd arrived safely.

Hi, Mum! I'm here, safe and sound and ready to turn in for the night. If you have a minute, can you hop onto that genealogy site and see what female person might have used that larger bedroom? I'm thinking it was Margaret, John's wife. Not sure where I'll start tomorrow with the cleaning and sorting. I'll figure that out when I wake up. I'll be in touch and send photos when I can.

Love you, Mum!

XO

She pulled the sofa closer to the fireplace, took a pillow from one of the chairs, and pulled her coat up around her. The warmth and soft crackling of the fire gently lifted tomorrow's list from her mind and set it aside until morning.

9

Chapter Nine

Paisley decided to start her cleaning odyssey in the drawing room on the main floor. It was one of the least cluttered rooms, she could meet with the inspector and appraiser there, and it was too chilly to do anything outside until whatever warmth the sun had to spare made it worth venturing out.

She found a tired, old vacuum cleaner in a corner closet and after emptying what looked like decades-old dirt, put it through its paces on the deep juniper and amber patterned rug. Until they could be properly cleaned, the matching drapes were brought outside the front door, given a good shake, and re-hung. Paisley remembered Finlay's gentle warning about being careful as she straddled two chairs and wrestled with the drapes. "There must be a ladder around here somewhere," she said to the empty room. "This really isn't the best way to do this."

Some of the paintings on the walls were portraits of individuals or carefully-posed couples; others were landscapes that looked like they could be locations on the property itself. Paisley was curious but didn't take the time to inspect them. She'd make time for that later. For now, they got a careful dusting along with the tables, the beautifully-carved mantle, and the oak bureau cabinet that opened to reveal a writing desk. The chair cushions received the same treatment as the drapes, while the attached upholstery received as good as a vacuuming as the old machine could muster. Paisley stood at the entrance to the room, happy with her efforts. One room done, how many to go?

The vestibule was smaller and easier. Sweep, dust, mop, and done. Same for the small water closet next door, except for the extra tasks of cleaning the toilet and sink. The aged vacuum's motor smelled like it had the tendency to overheat, so Paisley let it cool down in preparation for the dining room and study. It would never be able to handle the staircase, so she sat on the third step and ordered a new one online. The delivery confirmation said it would arrive Thursday or Friday. If it came Friday after she left for home, she could ask Finlay to stop by and set it somewhere safe and out of the weather for her.

When she returned to the study, she started a separate list for Finlay. Clean all chimneys. If he couldn't do it, he probably knew someone who could. She put together a cheese and lettuce sandwich for breakfast/lunch, grabbed her gloves and the box of yard bags, and ventured into the conservatory.

A weathered, stalwart rake leaned against the framework along with a shovel and a broom whose overworked bristles formed a stiff, diagonal wedge. Paisley worked around the still-dormant orange tree, carefully filling a large, plastic tub with pieces of the fallen glass panels before packing yard bags with the rest of the debris. She hefted the bags to the edge of the driveway along with a few, large branches that probably came from the towering sycamore nearby. After dragging the tub of broken ceiling panels halfway to the driveway, she envisioned new, replacement panels and wrestled the tub back against the inside wall of the conservatory.

It was satisfying to walk on the re-discovered flagstone pavers of the conservatory's interior after a careful, gentle raking to see what plants were there and determine if any were worth trying to salvage. January was the wrong time of year to make such a drastic decision, so she covered up some of the hopefuls; she'd wait until spring, then she could make a decision and safely prune the roses inside along with those clinging to the outside walls. She was sure her mum would want to dig in the dirt and lend her expertise to what was worth saving and decide what, if anything, should be discarded and replaced.

Paisley shook an unearthed scrap of burlap and wound it around the orange tree, hoping it would offer some protection from any cold nights yet to come. She took a photo of the cleaned-up conservatory and the rooms she cleaned and sent it to her mum.

Hi, Mum! Looks much better than when we first saw it! More rooms to clean. Will keep you posted. Hope all is well at home.

Love,

Paisley XO

The study and the dining room were fairly easy, like the drawing room. She'd clean the windows when the weather warmed up and she had a proper ladder. Opening the doors of a heavily-carved china cabinet revealed a full set of dishes and serving pieces; they were cream and white, gold-edged with a floral design and the name *Wedgwood* on the reverse side. The drawers in the midsection held heavily tarnished silverware, and in the lower section larger pieces were stored, like a soup tureen that matched the china and dulled, silver candelabras.

As she dusted the tabletop, she imagined how it would have looked set and ready to welcome evening dinner guests. Who would they have been? And even more important to her—who were the host and hostess?

She took a photo of the plate, a couple of the serving pieces, and a sample of the silverware pattern and sent them to Molly.

Look, Mum! An entire set of Wedgwood, plus serving pieces! Isn't it beautiful? Pretty silverware, too!

She made two mental notes as she left the room: 1) Find out how Mum was coming with the genealogy search, and 2) Text Finlay to see if he could bring her a takeaway meal when he came on Wednesday. The Silent Inn had her credit card information on file. She could call, place the order, and ask Finlay to bring it with him.

The downstairs was pretty much done, and the idea of a hot bath a tempting one. Paisley grabbed her bag and the tote of cleaning supplies and marched up the stairs. Should she sleep in the bedroom tonight? She hadn't cleaned or inspected it, but she could curl up with a blanket and at least have a well-deserved lie down.

First things first. Fingers crossed for a proper bath. After a few, resounding clunks from two floors down, hot water began to flow from the faucet into the oversized, claw-foot tub. Paisley quickly turned it off while she scrubbed and briskly rinsed it, unsure of the amount of hot water available. Grateful for its pristine condition, she put in the stopper and sat back on her heels as it filled and clouds of steam enveloped her in a warm, humid hug. As she slipped in, she wondered who else had relaxed and luxuriated here. Perhaps she'd find out later; it was her turn now.

Enough time passed to cool the water and transform Paisley's fingers into pale prunes; she had no idea how long she'd been asleep. After pulling on her flannel pyjamas, she opened the large, wooden wardrobe and looked for a blanket to curl up in until the bed could be changed and freshened in the morning.

The clothes were from sometime in the past, but Paisley wasn't exactly sure when. Crowded on the rod were blazers, a black print mini-dress, and blouses with puffing or gathering at the shoulders. She slid the hangers back and forth as best she could, but was too tired to take the time to inspect them. Tomorrow, or another time. What she was looking for was sitting on the shelf at the top—a neatly-folded, rose-colored wool blanket. Just what she needed. As she pulled it down, her hair caught on something that felt like a nail on the wood trim next to the door. "Ouch!" she said, wincing as she pulled her tangled hair free.

It *was* a nail, but what was hanging from it caused a catch in her breath and a joyful palpitation of her heart.

10

Chapter Ten

Paisley looked at the time on her phone. 8:30. The inspector and appraiser were coming at nine. She chastised herself for staying up too late last night inspecting and admiring the necklace she'd found on the nail in the wardrobe.

It was shaped like a flattened orb, framed in some sort of dull, silver metal that seemed to warm when Paisley held it in her hand. Beneath the glass on one side was a curvilinear letter P; that's what had made Paisley gasp when she first saw it. On the reverse was a mounting that held an oval, circular setting of a transparent, multi-faceted, deep-green stone.

She took a photo of it and sent a quick message to her mum.

Hi, Mum! Quick message – appraiser and inspector coming soon! Can you check the genealogy site to see if we have any female ancestors whose name started with the letter 'P' that might have worn this? Will call you later to let you know what happens today.

Love,

Paisley XO

Deodorant, teeth, hair. Put on something that wasn't terribly wrinkled or been worn before. Jeans and a sweatshirt would have to do. Paisley hurried through the routine, grabbed her phone, the binder it was sitting on, and hurried downstairs. There was only time for a refill of her water bottle before the crunching driveway gravel announced the arrival of the appraiser and inspector. She took a deep breath and whispered a prayer for luck and strength. *Please let this go well.*

"Good morning, gentlemen. Welcome to Thornberry Manor." It was a strange greeting, sounding more like a tour guide or a host for a special event. It was just as strange when they simultaneously held out their business cards to her. "Oh! Thank you." She looked at the names and then to their respective faces. "Jack Hunter, Appraiser and Mason Grant, Inspector. Come in, please." They passed through the vestibule, then Paisley turned to face them. "Where would you like to start?"

* * *

It was almost noon when their vehicles retreated along the lake and out of sight. Paisley knew it was part of the process, but their poking, prodding, and questions felt intrusive. Despite the short time she'd been at Thornberry, she'd grown quite protective of it. As she escorted them to the driveway, they assured her they would be submitting reports—hopefully within a week's time.

She leaned against the securely-locked door with a sigh of relief while her rumbling stomach reminded her she hadn't eaten since last night. The nearly-empty refrigerator in the kitchen held the last of the cheese, two apples, and the parchment-wrapped, sliced turkey. "I guess it'll be another soup and sandwich day," she announced to the dimly-lit space. *I should probably tackle this room next.* After sweeping, mopping, and wiping everything down, she'd write up an inventory and send photos to her mum. She'd like that.

Paisley slowly circled the kitchen as she ate her sandwich, peeking into the nooks and crannies and craning her neck for a look up the massive fireplace's chimney. The bowl holding her soup was part of a large set of sturdy earthenware dishes probably used by servants or staff at some point in the manor's past.

She sent photos and a text to her mum but didn't expect to hear back until after the bookshop closed for the day. Had she had a chance to research any female ancestors whose name began with the letter 'P'? As she climbed the stairs from the kitchen to the ground floor, she thought about the cemetery a short distance away from the western side of the house. There was still plenty of daylight to explore it and see what was there. Perhaps a clue or even an answer.

She pulled on her mac and zipped it up against the late afternoon chill. It felt good to get outside, even if it was under a heavy, grey sky. The leaves and litter under her feet released a damp, earthy scent; the ground was feeding itself in anticipation of spring. Here and there a flagstone revealed itself, encouraging Paisley to reveal all of them with the rake. The stone wall was solid and sturdy, and with some gentle wrenching, she managed to open the iron entrance gate.

It wasn't huge by any means, but Paisley wasn't sure

where to start. *There must have been some rhyme or reason to the layout, but I guess it really doesn't matter. It'll be easy enough to figure out by the dates and names—I hope.* She decided to tackle it gradually, quietly, and with respect by walking along the inside of the wall, occasionally running her hand along the rough, worn surface and crevices cushioned with moss and lichen. The tall grass flattened behind her and rested in random places on the ground where the wind and rain had gotten the better of it.

There were no elaborate monuments, but there was one, large combined stone in the center that caught Paisley's attention. There were two people named on the stone; Paisley took a photo of it as an easy reminder of the dates and something she could send to her mum. These were her ancestors, and she would hopefully find them on the ancestry site.

Lord Flemon Hix was listed first, with dates of 1804-1856. Next to him was his wife Polly, with dates 1809-1858. Pushing aside the tangle of vegetation to her right, she discovered uncovered the name of their daughter, Phoebe Hix, 1827-1847. Paisley gasped. "Hello there! Could the necklace have been yours? Passed on to you by your mother?"

Ignoring for a moment the month and day, she stood and did some calculations on her phone; Flemon died at 52, Polly at 49. That seemed to be a logical lifespan for people during the Victorian period. But Phoebe died when she was just 20. What happened? Illness? Injury? Maybe they could find some documents that would solve the mystery. A dark cloud ushered in a freezing, spitting rain that tapped against the stones and dry, brittle foliage at her feet. As Paisley turned away, something else on Phoebe's stone made her drop to her knees and quickly rub at the writing.

There was another set of dates and another name below hers, written in smaller letters–Primrose. Underneath, the dates revealed the heartbreaking event. June 23, 1847–June 23, 1847. Paisley glanced at Phoebe's date of death—it was the same as little Primrose. Phoebe most likely died in childbirth, and Primrose did not survive, either.

As she rose, she whispered a prayer for them. The ancestry records might show Phoebe's existence, but Paisley wasn't sure about Primrose. She'd need to ask her mum.

The rain shifted from spitting to a steady, chilling shower. Exploring the rest of the cemetery would have to wait until the weather allowed her back. She left the gate ajar; there was no point in putting additional strain on it and risk damaging it beyond repair. The dirt beneath it could be moved aside, and the task of fixing it would be added to the growing list for Finlay.

11

Chapter Eleven

After a hot bath and doing makeshift laundry in the kitchen sink, Paisley looked over her meager dinner choices. They were getting ridiculously slim. Another soup and sandwich meal—really? What she wouldn't give for something else, like pizza, shepherd's pie, or fish and chips. Tomorrow, she'd ask Finlay to bring something for both of them and charge it to her credit card at the Silent Inn.

The sound of a honking horn sent her scrambling up the stairs, hoping it was Finlay with some sort of divine intervention dinner replacement. She was happy to see him and grateful that he had a substantial-looking takeaway bag in his hand. "You're a sight for sore eyes," she said as she held the door open for him. "And thanks for whatever it is that you brought to eat. My menu choices are getting quite limited." His dark, wavy hair was tousled by the wind, and the warmth in his deep, blue eyes told her he was happy he'd made the decision to visit her. "I need to pay you for this," she said, pointing at the bag.

"Tonight, dinner is on me." He passed through the vestibule and looked around. "You've been busy. It's looking so much better."

"Thanks. Amazing, what manual labor can accomplish." She extended her arm to the drawing room. "Should we eat in here? The dining room is so formal, and the kitchen is dark and dreary this late in the day." No, the kitchen wouldn't do; she dreaded the thought of Finlay seeing her laundry strung up from window to hearth.

"Fine with me." He set the bag down on the table in front of the fireplace. "How about a fire to take away the chill?"

"Oh, that would be great, thanks." Paisley opened the bag and inhaled deeply. The aroma of beef, potatoes, and gravy wafted up. "It smells delicious, whatever it is."

"I thought shepherd's pie would be a fitting choice on a wet, grey day like this. And Olivia included some other goodies, like blackberry crumble for dessert." He looked at what Paisley was unpacking. "I think she sent some scones for tomorrow's breakfast, too."

"That was so thoughtful of her, and you, to collect and deliver this to me."

Finlay had a small fire going, but it wouldn't last long. "Be right back," he announced. "I think there might be some larger pieces of wood laying around outside. I'll see what I can find." After feeding the fire, he settled into the chair opposite her and tucked into his own order of shepherd's pie. "So, what news from the appraiser and inspector?"

"Well, some things were not a surprise, like the electrical and boiler. The water will have to be tested along with the age and functioning of the pump." Paisley looked around. "Windows and the roof. No leaks yet, but the roof is old, and new windows will make it more energy efficient."

"It sounds like you're considering keeping the place."

Chewing the food in her mouth gave Paisley time to formulate her response. She held up a finger, then dabbed her mouth with her napkin. "Well, the property legally belongs to my mum now, and we're trying to find the best way forward. She's a bit overwhelmed by it all, but I think there are possibilities worth exploring." She hesitated before continuing. "The appraisal needs to be under £325,000 to avoid paying inheritance tax. That would be a huge help. And I've written about getting a historic grant to cover some of the repairs and renovations. They won't cover anything done prior to being approved, so I'm at a standstill with any major work until they look at my application."

"When are the reports from the appraiser and inspector supposed to be ready?"

"They promised next week. In the meantime, I can clean and sort and get outside when the weather warms up."

"I'd be happy to lend a hand."

"I appreciate the offer, but I can't afford to pay anyone…"

Finlay held his hand up and gently interrupted her. "I'm not asking to get paid. If you get the grant money, and there are certain things it will cover, then we can talk. Until then, consider it free labor."

"Why would you bother? You have your job at the Silent Inn and your other paying customers."

Finlay crumpled his napkin, tossed it into the fire, and leaned back in the chair. It was the perfect excuse for Paisley to study his handsome features while she waited for him to speak. "There aren't many properties left like Thornberry Manor. I've seen it age and suffer from neglect over the years, and I think it deserves to be saved. Perhaps it can find a new life as a vacation destination or a place for retreats and family gatherings. Unlike years in the past, it needs to pay its own way, and people are finding creative ways to make that happen."

Paisley leaned forward and thrust her arms out into the air. "Yes! I've had some of those same ideas! Mum thinks I'm crazy, but I think it could work." She looked around the room, then back at him. "There's so much to do, but I can start out doing a lot of what a grant won't cover, like cleaning, sorting, and getting trash hauled away. That would go a long way in getting things started."

"So far, so good." Finlay rose from the chair and put the used take away containers back in the bag. "I'll take care of this—you have enough trash to deal with already, and we don't need bugs or critters coming around."

Paisley laughed. "You're right." She walked him to the door and leaned against the frame, wishing he wasn't leaving so soon. "You'll be here sometime tomorrow?"

"Yes. I have tomorrow off, so why don't you text me a list tonight or in the morning and let me know what needs to be done and what you need. I'll bring a ladder for sure and my tools."

"I'm not sure why you're jumping in to help me, but I'm very grateful."

Finlay turned and moved one step closer to Paisley.

"Like I told you—this manor house deserves a new lease on life." His voice lowered to barely above a whisper. "And I like you, Paisley. Plain and simple. I like you, and I want to help you." He reached for the door latch and winked at her as he pulled the door closed. "See you in the morning."

"Goodnight," she answered to the firmly snapped latch. "Thanks for coming by and for dinner." Had he heard her? She didn't want to open the door just to say goodnight and start another conversation—that would be weird. She liked Finlay, but it would have been awkward and somewhat juvenile to return the sentiment by saying, "I like you, too." It would be better for everyone if she kept the warm feelings for him to herself. For now, anyway.

12

Chapter Twelve

Paisley had some time in the morning before Finlay showed up, so she decided to deal with the bedroom she'd been staying in. Her mum had been busy on the ancestry site and told her that the bedroom furnishings and contents probably belonged to John's wife Margaret who passed away in 2000. *Was there a gravestone for them in the cemetery?* She hadn't seen one on her last visit; when she got the chance, she'd take a proper tour.

Armed with a box of trash bags, she began emptying the contents of the bureau and set aside the breakables to be

74

boxed up separately. It could all be donated, the room given a thorough cleaning, and redecorated with something more contemporary and to her taste. She smiled in her mind; the fate of the property was still uncertain, but she'd already come to think of Thornberry Manor as hers. Well, her mother's, then hers. As she finished emptying the wardrobe, the mirrored, inside of the door remained ajar and reflected the image of the necklace sitting on the bedside table.

Paisley scooped it up and held it to the light, studying the filigree letter 'P' and the green stone as it spun slowly in front of her. The silver chain was long enough to slip over her head without unhooking the clasp. As it settled around her neck, it felt warm on her skin, the flattened orb resting comfortably on her chest between the base of her throat and the top of her breasts.

When she turned back to the mirror, the warmth intensified, coursing like a fever throughout her entire body. Her muscles felt like liquid caramel, and the room blurred and swirled like a carousel ride around her. Paisley didn't know if she deliberately sat or fell to the floor, but when the room stopped spinning, she knew something in her world had changed.

It was hard to breathe. As the room settled down and the dizziness subsided, Paisley realized the reason for her breathing difficulty was the fact that she was wearing a corset under what felt like layers of clothing and a muted, floral print dress she'd never seen before. It was floor-length with long sleeves and a full skirt, its neckline hiding the necklace around her neck.

As she walked around the room, she realized that she was in the same bedroom, which meant she was still at Thornberry Manor. But it was altogether changed. The familiar wardrobe was there, but full of unfamiliar clothes. The slumbering fireplace looked familiar, although it had a fresher, younger face and a mantle with candlesticks at each end and a display of porcelain figurines between them.

The bed and other furnishings were unlike any Paisley had ever seen. Heavy, burgundy drapes framed the window that was covered by an ivory lace panel. The same, rich burgundy covered the loveseat in the corner and the deep red was part of the patterned rug on the floor.

The bed was dark, heavy, and beautiful; Paisley wondered what had happened to it, the matching bureau, and bedside table. She would have loved them in the room that had been Margaret's—the one she was staying in. But wasn't this it—the same room?

The now-familiar sound of crunching gravel on the drive drew her to the window. Was it Finlay? As she pulled back the curtain she gasped, realizing it couldn't possibly be him. The only mode of transportation appeared to be on horseback or horse-drawn carriage, and the guests and servants were dressed in clothes from a distant past. The grounds were beautifully maintained, and the lake beyond was as she remembered. She was at Thornberry Manor, but not in the present. What present? Wasn't she in the present? She was pretty sure she wasn't in 2024 anymore. If it wasn't 2024, what year was it?

A gentle tap on the door jolted Paisley's thoughts, forcing her to whirl around, smoothing her skirt as a female servant entered and greeted her. "Mornin', Miss. I'm sorry to interrupt. I'm here to tidy your room." Paisley studied her uniform as she moved to tie back the curtains; it consisted of a dark dress with white cuffs and collar and a white apron and hat. "I thought all of the guests would be downstairs by now—shall I come back later?"

Paisley smiled and felt the need to introduce herself but refrained from extending her hand. She also decided it would be wise to use her mum's maiden name as her surname. "Good morning. I'm Paisley Hicks."

"I'm Hettie, Miss. Pleasure to have you visit Thornberry Manor. I believe you'll find most everyone in the drawing room or the conservatory." She looked around the room, then back at Paisley. "Is there anything I can get you?"

"No, thank you, Hettie. I'll just make my way

downstairs." The passageway she faced after closing the bedroom door was both strange and familiar. The floor plan of the house was the same, but the décor and furnishings were definitely from some other time. *How am I going to figure out what year it is without sounding like an idiot? And how am I going to explain my presence here?*

With a nod, she greeted several other maids who were busy cleaning the upstairs rooms; one of the small carts in the hallway held clothes she supposed needed to be laundered and a pair of men's shoes to be shined. On the upper shelf of the cart was a used brandy snifter, the empty bottle, and a newspaper. Paisley slowed her pace until the maid returned to the room, then plucked the paper from the cart and tucked it discreetly under her arm. When she reached the upholstered bench on the stair landing, she sat and unfolded it, eagerly looking at the top for a date. There it was, in a bold, attention-getting type: **JANUARY 27, 1829**.

As her eyes remained fixed on the date, a conversation from the floor below floated up the stairwell and settled on the seat next to her. "Have you seen him? Such a beautiful baby!" one voice exclaimed. Someone answered, a bit more hushed. "Flemon must be delighted to have a son at last—Polly has finally fulfilled her duty."

Paisley committed the two names to memory. On the way down the last flight of stairs, she scoured her brain for a family name she could use when she was introduced. *I should have gone to the graveyard for names or asked Mum.* No matter. She'd have to figure it out on her own now. The hum of conversation increased as she moved toward the drawing room; most of the women were clustered in one corner of the room, hovering around a young woman seated and proudly displaying an infant.

Paisley entered and stood off to the side, scanning the room she'd just cleaned and shared takeaway in with Finlay. She decided to introduce herself as Paisley Hicks and explain that she was a distant relative from the southern part of England, travelling with family who were unfortunately attending to other business and unable to visit. What branch of the Hicks family was she? She'd explain that the connection was on her mother's side; that wouldn't be as relevant to the men, and they would be less likely to question or investigate.

She smiled as a matronly-looking woman approached her. "I don't think we've been introduced." She extended a jeweled, arthritic hand. "My name is Audrey Hix. I am aunt to young Polly seated over there with her new son, Henry." Just then, a young girl with curly, flaxen hair, perhaps two years old, scampered past them and ran up to Polly and the baby. "That little tempest is Phoebe, her daughter."

Paisley gently took her hand in hers. "It's a pleasure to meet you. My name is Paisley Hicks. My family is from the Isle of Wight but travelling north on business. While their business demands that they be elsewhere, they brought me here to call on the family and pay our respects to the new, little one."

Audrey extended her arm toward Polly and the others. "Come. I'll introduce you."

Polly looked younger than her by several years, at least. Maybe in her early twenties. And two children already? That's the way they did it then. Find a husband, marry well, and have children. Preferably sons—to carry on the name, inherit the land holdings, and father more sons. Daughters were an afterthought, something akin to serving dessert after a meal; they were an expensive indulgence to enjoy after the main course was complete. Polly had managed it, even if Phoebe had come first; all of the pressure for women to produce sons really made no sense, since men were the ones who determined the sex of the baby. Nothing would be gained by explaining that fact. It would only arouse suspicion and raise questions about her presence, not to mention her knowledge of X and Y chromosomes they knew nothing about and she was not prepared to answer.

Paisley smiled as she approached Polly, Phoebe, and the baby. Audrey made the introduction, and Polly graciously acknowledged her. Weariness was masked with fine clothes, jewellery, and carefully controlled tresses the color of Phoebe's, but her hazel eyes begged desperately for a nap. "It's a pleasure to meet you," she spoke, barely above a whisper. Her intention was not to wake the baby, but his blue eyes opened and studied her. She proudly shifted him so that Paisley could see him to better advantage. "This is my son, Henry James."

He *was* a beautiful baby, with hair darker than his mother's that looked like it would either wave or curl when it grew longer. Paisley guessed he was just a few days old. "When was he born?"

Polly stroked his cheek. "On the 20th of January." His cheeks were rosy and full; wherever the wet nurse was, she was doing an excellent job. As little Henry squirmed, Paisley noticed a small, brown birthmark under his left ear; it was shaped like a small, chocolate comma. Either wet or hungry, or both, Henry let out a howl that silenced the room. "Fetch Annabelle," she ordered Phoebe in a hissing, hushed whisper.

Demanding instant gratification, Henry kicked and flung his arms into the air with such unexpected force that he slid from Polly's lap and would have hit the floor if Paisley hadn't caught him on the way down. She hoisted him over her shoulder and patted his back as Polly watched with shocked relief. "There, Master Henry. Annabelle will be here soon, and all will be well."

As conversation resumed in the room, Annabelle materialized at her side, lifted Henry from her shoulder, and whisked him out of the room. As he left with one last howl, Paisley thought about the date she'd seen on the newspaper. Henry was a mere seven days old, and any daily newspaper in London could take days or weeks to reach Thornberry Manor. Perhaps it was hand-carried from London by a guest. However it had arrived, it was the year that Paisley's memory latched onto—1829.

13

Chapter Thirteen

Paisley circulated around the room as discreetly as possible, nodding and greeting the other guests as she encountered them. After smiles and introductions, she decided that the study might be a good place to observe without being drawn into too much conversation. As she entered, she noticed Polly's husband Flemon talking to a woman holding a book in her hand.

"Ah! Miss Hicks!" Flemon beckoned for her to join him and the woman in the somber, earthy-brown dress. "Audrey tells me you're a distant relative our family has met for the first time today." He turned back to the quiet woman, his blue eyes sparkling and his rotund chest swelling with pride. "I'd like to present Mary Shelley, the famous author of a great many works."

Paisley's hand went to her chest, covering the warm, rounded orb. She extended her other hand to Mary, doing all she could to maintain her composure. Mary was tall, with a fair complexion, oval-shaped face, and dark, chestnut hair pulled away from her face into a soft, conservative style. Her brown eyes were soft and kind but held the look of someone who'd endured much pain and heartache in her life.

"Do you know of her work?" Flemon asked as he stroked his salt-and-pepper beard.

Mary looked at Paisley for an answer, and Paisley nodded, squeaking out a feeble, "Yes."

"Which one are you most familiar with?" she asked.

"Oh, *Frankenstein*, to be sure," Paisley responded, her voice barely above a whisper. "It's a fascinating, unusual, and multi-faceted story. I've read it several times."

"Do you have your own copy?"

"No. I borrowed one from a friend." If borrowing meant she'd checked out a copy from the library as a child, and the library was also her friend, then she was telling the truth.

"Well, we can remedy that right now. I have an extra

copy in my room. I'll give that one to Flemon and Polly, and you can have this one."

Paisley gasped, then looked at Mary without trying to appear starstruck. "Would you be willing to sign it for me?"

"I would be happy to." She moved to the desk, found ink and quill, and signed the inside title page.

"Thank you ever so much, Mrs. Shelley. I will treasure it always." Paisley held out her hand to shake Mary's one, last time. "It's a great honor to meet you."

"The pleasure is mine, Paisley."

Flemon ended the encounter by announcing that there were others who wanted to meet Mary. Paisley held her breath and the book to her chest as she watched Mary leave the study and join the others in the drawing room. *Her book is one we had on the feature table at the bookshop.* Paisley watched in awe as Mary interacted with others in the next room. How could she know; how could any of them know that Mary's work would be treasured by readers almost two-hundred years in the future? That *Frankenstein* would be a monster character in films, costumes, and even breakfast cereal? Paisley sank into the desk chair, trying to take it all in.

Her thoughts were interrupted by the voice of someone speaking to her. "I'm sorry, what?"

It was Polly. "I was inquiring after the length of your stay. How long will you be with us?" Her words were sincere, but the tone was less welcoming. Did she perceive Paisley as some sort of threat? An unwelcome guest? Was she overwhelmed by the extravagant social event that came with the birth of a son?

Paisley hadn't thought about how to leave—or even if she *could* return to her own time. The answer to that seemed tied to the necklace she was wearing. If she waited until evening, it would be easier to slip away unnoticed. "I believe they'll be returning for me this evening, and we have lodging in the village." Paisley rose from the chair, still clutching the book to her chest. "I'd like to venture outside if you don't mind."

"You'll need a shawl. Did you bring one with you?"

"It's probably upstairs, but don't worry on my account. I'll be fine. Thank you just the same." With a smile, a bob of her head, and a half-curtsy, Paisley made her way to the conservatory where she hoped there would be doors leading outside. Three steps down, and she was among the moist, earthy scent of plants and trees. The glass ceiling was beautiful and intact; its curved, etched panels were the same fragments she'd carefully gathered just a day or two earlier. She made a mental note to try and have them replicated for the repair.

Guests of various ages took advantage of the beautiful, green space, seated at small clusters of wrought-iron chairs and tables placed among the ferns and young rose bushes that were too fragile to venture outdoors. Pots of purple and yellow pansies bobbed their heads and offered up their sweet scent to anyone willing to pause long enough to appreciate them. A long, wooden table at the far end under a bank of windows held trays of soil and seeds that hadn't yet sprouted; perhaps these plants were for a kitchen garden.

With her self-guided tour concluded, Paisley ventured out to explore the grounds. The chatter of smoking men around the carriages and horses in the front of the house prompted her to go in the opposite direction. Across a small expanse of lawn was the flagstone walkway leading to the walled-in cemetery. Paisley decided not to visit; it might seem too bold and forward to be caught exploring such an intimate and private space, even if it was her ancestors who were buried there.

The back of the house was more informal and park-like, with a kitchen garden, lawn, and trees that were given license to grow where nature intended. The gravel drive encircled the house with a back entry for servants and deliveries. A few servants were seated at the wooden, trestle table outside the door, eating lunch, visiting, and/or smoking. Paisley would have been more comfortable joining this group than those that were in the drawing room and conservatory. They knew how the real world worked and what was going on behind the scenes. But her dress and apparent position immediately set her apart from them; they looked at her with polite suspicion as she nodded and continued walking. She pretended to read her book as she moved away from them, circling back to the west side of the house and the stream that fed the lake in front.

Polly's question about her length of stay brought her thoughts back to when she should leave, *if* she *could* leave. Would it be as simple as removing the necklace? If so, where and when? Evening would probably be best, when most of the house would be asleep. She could leave a note that Hettie could deliver in the morning; something about her family arriving late to retrieve her and not wanting to disturb her in the late evening hours. Paisley nodded to herself. Yes, that was a good plan. In the meantime, she'd explore as much of the house as she could so her mind could compare 1829 with 2024.

It was fun and scary at the same time—sneaking around in her own house. Feeling braver and more adventurous, she ducked, sat, and pretended to be reading while she waited for her chance to explore the dining room, study (again), and the rooms upstairs. She pretended to be lost when she ventured down into the kitchen but got a chance to visit with some of the staff and was offered a plate of bread and cheese and a mug of cider.

When the shadows deepened and slanted low through the windows, she returned to her room, composed the letter that Hettie would deliver to Flemon and Polly, and hid in the wardrobe when she was summoned for dinner. As the footsteps faded away, she emerged and quickly studied the room, willing her memory to retain all that it had seen. She quickly and carefully left the letter on the bedside table where she knew Hettie would find and deliver it.

There was no more to be done, no reason to stay without drawing suspicion. Paisley looked around the room one, last time as she sat on the bed. Clutching the book to her chest, she slowly removed the necklace and slipped it into the pocket of her skirt. The warm, melty feeling returned, and Paisley felt herself fall back onto the bed.

14

Chapter Fourteen

Before she opened her eyes, Paisley knew she was back. It was the present-day scent drifting around that confirmed it—floating past the presence of antique, wooden furniture and floor wax was her favorite scent of lemon window cleaner. But her body was reluctant to move. The muscle aches and weakness reminded Paisley of recovering from a bad case of the flu. Even her eyelids hurt when she opened them. Best to stay put and stay still for now. She drifted back to sleep until the ring tone on her phone forced her to reach over and answer it.

Her brain struggled to settle on the day and time. Paisley looked at the screen on her phone. It was still Wednesday and about the same time as it was before she'd donned the necklace. So, no time had passed in the present, but Paisley was sure that wasn't the case in 1829. She'd spent the better part of the day at the Thornberry Manor of the past and returned at nightfall. It would appear that present-day time stopped (and waited for her?) when she traveled but proceeded at a normal pace in the past.

"I'm standing outside your door. I knocked a few times but you didn't answer. Are you okay and just want to be left alone?" There was a pause on the line. "I just stopped by to see if you needed anything."

It took a while for the name *Finlay* on the screen to register before she responded. "If you can give me a couple of minutes, I'll be down as soon as I can." Her legs gave out once and nearly again before she was able to stand on her own. Reaching into the pocket of her jeans to remove the necklace, she felt the chain, the oval orb, and hard, prickly crumbs. She carefully set the orb and chain on the bedside table, surprised that the glass and curvilinear letter 'P' beneath it were still intact and unbroken. The crumbs turned out to be the remnants of the green stone set in the reverse side—what she'd thought might be an emerald. Slowly pulling her pocket inside out, she brushed the crumbs onto a small dish and straightened her clothes as best she could. She'd deal with the shattered stone later.

The book! She gasped, patting herself and the space around her on the bed. Where was the book she'd clutched to her chest as she slipped the necklace off for her return? Paisley looked around frantically, but there was no book. "No," she moaned, resigning herself to the thought that items from the past were not intended to journey with her to the future. Steadying herself against the doorframe, she took a deep breath and weaving like a drunken party-goer, made her way to the stairs.

She made it as far as the landing before a wave of dizziness forced her to sit on the upholstered bench, taking deep breaths and dipping her head between her knees. It was the same bench where she'd sat and found the 1829 date on the newspaper taken from the maid's cart. *Did that really happen? Of course, it did! It wasn't a dream or an imagining. Somehow, it had really happened.*

By the time she reached the bottom of the stairs and opened the door, beads of sweat had popped up on her forehead, and her entire body felt flushed and feverish. She leaned against the open door in an effort to dispel the white, flickering light behind her eyes that signaled she was about to faint.

Finlay caught her as she slid to the floor and carried

her into the drawing room. He settled her into one of the chairs and knelt in front of her. "What happened, Paisley? Are you ill? Have you had anything to eat or drink today?" He motioned for her to stay put. "I've got some water and snacks in the truck. Don't move."

Before she had a chance to respond he was gone, then back with a bottle of water and a raspberry scone. He knelt again, then sat back on his heels as he handed her one, then the other. Waiting patiently, he watched for the color to return to Paisley's cheeks. "Better?"

Paisley nodded. "I'm not sure what happened." She hated lying, but the truth was beyond explaining right now. "Guess I've been trying to do too much too soon."

"You're returning to Bonchurch on Friday, right?" Paisley nodded. "So, you have today and tomorrow. Is there anything that you feel *has* to be done before you return home?"

Paisley shifted in the chair and looked around her. "I was working on the bedroom I've been staying in, but that can wait." She took another sip of water. "Maybe we can take a walk around, and we'll see what seems to be the most urgent."

"Whenever you feel you're up to it."

Paisley took Finlay's hand, and he helped her to her feet. She felt better; still a bit wobbly, but perhaps moving about would help her body adjust. "Let's start upstairs, then I can grab a jacket before we go outside."

He paused as she caught her breath at the landing, then they moved to the bedroom she'd been using. She pointed to the bags and boxes in one corner. "All of that is going to be donated, but there will be more, I'm sure." When he moved toward the bedside table, she tried to discreetly place herself between him and the necklace. She didn't even want to think about explaining what had happened; she was still trying to wrap her own mind around it.

They took their time moving through each of the upstairs rooms. Paisley hesitated in each as flashbacks from earlier furnishings and decorations swept through. She hoped Finlay interpreted her pausing as her conducting a mental inventory of what needed to be done. "I'll let you know as soon as I hear from the inspector. Then we can come up with a plan, but I can't do anything major now in case I'm approved for the Historic England grant. Everything that's done prior to approval won't be covered, so I'm restricted to basic cleanup and things that aren't too costly—things I can do on my own."

They returned to the main level where recent memories of the past threatened to reveal themselves if Paisley wasn't careful. They went into the study where she'd met Mary Shelley and been gifted the recently lost, autographed copy of *Frankenstein*, then to the drawing room where she'd met Flemon and Polly Hix, the 1829 owners of Thornberry Manor. She could almost hear little Phoebe's laughter and feel the soft, wriggling of Henry's body in her arms.

The kitchen was intact for the most part, but Paisley was sure the inspector would have something to say about the age of the wiring and the plumbing. She pushed that to the back of her mind. *One disaster at a time, and pray for a grant.* "I think my greatest concern is here," she told Finlay as they entered the conservatory. "I did as much as I could, but the roof concerns me. Is there any way we can cover it, even with tarps, to keep the weather out until we hear about the grant?"

She thought about the pansies, the roses waiting to move outside, and the laughter and conversation of the clusters of visitors enjoying the warm, green space when she had last been here. Except for her and Finlay's footsteps on the flagstones, it was silent now—dormant, chilly, and neglected. Maybe its time would come again. Aside from the damage that needed to be repaired, it looked much better than it had when she first arrived. There was hope. "If I called in a takeaway order from the inn, would you be willing to deliver and share it with me?"

"How about I take you to the inn for dinner? Maybe

you need to take a break and get away for an evening."

"That's a really nice offer, but I'm not feeling up to it today."

Finlay took her hand and gave it a gentle squeeze. "I understand. Totally."

"I wanted to finish getting the bedroom that I've been using sorted and bagged up. Then a bath and maybe a nap. By that time, you'll probably be back with dinner. Have Olivia put it on my credit card, and I owe you for petrol. You've been making a lot of trips up here to help me."

Finlay responded to her financial concerns with a smile. "What would you like for dinner?" Finlay pulled out his phone and showed her the menu on the inn's app.

Paisley leaned into him and scanned it with her finger. He felt safe, warm, and secure, and she found the light touch of his arm around her comforting. "Oh, fish and chips sounds really good. And how about blackberry crumble for dessert?"

"And to drink?"

"Hmm…Surprise me. Anything but water. That's all I've been drinking for the past few days."

He gave her shoulders a squeeze, then stepped away. "Tell you what. I'm going to leave now and load up a tarp and whatever else I can find to secure the conservatory as best we can. We can work on that tomorrow. Then I'll pick up our dinner order. I'll text you when I'm on my way. Sound like a plan?"

"It sounds like the perfect plan. Thank you, Finlay, for all of your help. You've done so much already; I can't pay you much now, but if I get that grant, I'll find a way to reimburse you for everything and pay you for your time." The hug she gave him was quick and somewhat awkward; neither of them was expecting it. Her cheeks felt warm, and she knew it had nothing to do with her recent return from 1829.

"You sure you're okay?" The expression on Finlay's face was a combination of concern and genuine affection.

"I'm fine. Really." Just then, the phone in her pocket rang. "My mum. I better have a chat with her, bring her up to speed. See you later, Finlay."

Paisley closed the conservatory door, gently patted the dormant orange tree, and climbed the stairs to the landing. Sitting on the bench, she changed the mode to FaceTime. "Hi, Mum! How are you and things at the bookshop?"

"It's all good here. Tell me what you've been up to."

"Cleaning and sorting," she answered as she continued up the stairs to her room. "I'll take pictures to show you when I get home." She sat on the bed and tossed aside yesterday's clothes. "Remember Finlay? Our driver?

He's bringing supper later, and tomorrow we're going to secure the conservatory as best we can. Then he'll bring me to the train station on Friday."

Paisley's hand strayed enough for Molly to see the necklace on the bedside table. "What is that, Paisley? Turn your phone back to the table again." Paisley swung the phone over the necklace, then back to her face. "You'll never believe it, Mum, but it's too hard to explain over the phone. I'll bring it with me and explain when I get home."

15

Chapter Fifteen

Paisley woke to the sound of tires crunching on the gravel drive and Finlay's truck door slamming. She scrambled out of bed, opened the window, and called down to him. "Sorry! I'm slow getting started. I'll be down as soon as I can."

Finlay looked up and smiled. "Mornin' Paisley. I'll just start unloading." He held up a bag and a thermos bottle. "Tea and scones! I was pretty sure you wouldn't have taken the time to eat anything."

"Thanks, Finlay. You're the best."

"You know it."

He gave her a hug when she met him outside the conservatory and handed her a scone and mug of tea. Paisley liked his hugs, the feel of him. His affection was comforting and gave Paisley a warm, secure feeling. "So, how are we going to tackle this?"

"Well, I'll get on the roof where it meets the rest of the building and roll the tarp over the open spaces. Then we'll secure it from the sides and tie it down where the grommets are."

Paisley looked at the conservatory space under the skeletal framework. "I need to move some stuff around down here in case something else falls." She pointed to the tub of broken, glass panels she'd gathered from the flagstone floor. "Is there someone we can take these to and see if they can replicate them? I know we'll need to repair or replace the framework, but I'm hoping the glass people can help us figure out how strong the framework has to be. Maybe there's an alternative to this heavy glass." She held a fragment in her hand, then handed it to him.

"I think we can look at acrylic or polycarbonate, but you'd want the same design, right?" He looked through the pieces in the box. "Why don't you see if you can find enough to have a complete example? Then we can take those to the glass guy in Keighley."

"Good plan. I knew you'd be able to figure it out, Finlay."

"It's what I do, Paisley. I solve problems, and I fix things."

While Finlay positioned the ladder, Paisley hurried to move anything that might get damaged if pieces of glass or framework should fall. Last, she dragged the orange tree next to the stairs leading to the drawing room. "You'll be safe here, I promise."

Turns out, they were a good team. They worked well together, solving the problems that came up, anticipating the next step, and handling frustration with laughter instead of profanity. A couple of hours later, Finlay stood on the ground in front of the conservatory entrance. "I think we've got it, barring any severe storms or heavy snow." He turned to Paisley. "Now, how about we go into town for something to eat? I'm pretty sure you don't feel like cooking, and I sure don't. Besides, I wonder what food, if any, you have left."

"Sure—if you let me buy."

"Deal."

"Let me get the first layer of grime off, anyway."

"Sure. I'll load up and wash a bit down in the kitchen."

Paisley hurried up the stairs, did a quick wash, and put on clean jeans and a burgundy jumper. She didn't bother fixing her makeup but teased the snarls out of her russet curls. That was enough; she didn't want to appear too eager.

She was pleasantly surprised at how clean and organized the interior of Finlay's truck was. Those she'd passed by or were parked near the bookshop on occasions were a maelstrom of receipts, food wrappers, and beverage containers partially-submerged in months' worth of sand and debris on the floor mats. There was some sand, but the seats were clean enough to sit on without worry of jam or spilled tea soaking into the backside of one's pants.

Finlay closed the narrow, partitioned file box that held his paperwork and tucked it in the space behind his seat. "That gives us a bit more room and puts an end to the workday."

Paisley settled comfortably into the seat. "So, tell me something about yourself, Finlay Wood. Do you have family? Do they live nearby? What do you like to do when you're not working for the Silent Inn, your other jobs, or helping at Thornberry Manor?"

He glanced uncomfortably at her.

"What? You know plenty about me, my family, and the whole Thornberry Manor saga." She smoothed her jumper and looked out the window as she calculated her next response. "I like to have some background information on the people I hire to work on my property."

Finlay burst out laughing. "First of all, it's technically your mum's property. Second, have you relegated me to the status of employee? Really, Paisley, I thought we were past that."

"You're right, Mr. Wood. I think we are." She tried to keep a straight face, but it was no good. She giggled, then laughed as Finlay grabbed her hand and kissed it.

"You're a piece of work, Paisley Venne. Truly, you are."

"I've been called worse."

Finlay pulled into the parking lot of the Silent Inn. "Let's get seated and order, then I'll tell you what you want to know."

They greeted Olivia and Lewis and visited with them over a pint about work on Thornberry Manor and goings on in the village. They ordered bangers and mash and quietly tucked away a few mouthfuls before coming up for air. "This is so good. I didn't realize how hungry I was."

"Me neither." Finlay finished chewing, set his fork and knife down, and took a significant sip of ale. He wiped his mouth and leaned back in his chair. "So, a bit about me. I live in Keighley, but you probably knew that from my business card. I have a small place not far from here; makes it handy to work here, and I try to take outside jobs that aren't too far away. Every now and again one comes along that involves staying out of town, but I try to limit them unless the money is too good to turn down."

Paisley leaned forward, elbows on the table, and chin in her hands. "Family? Significant other?"

"Well, if you know me at all, you'd know there isn't a significant other. If there was, I would have been keeping things on a strictly business level." He shifted in his chair, clearly uncomfortable with the topic. "Sure, I've dated and had a couple of relationships that I thought might evolve into something, but looking back, I can see it would never have worked out with them."

"Now, about my family. My father, Nick, passed about five years ago. Cancer. My mum Hazel lives in Keighley in her own little flat close enough so I can check on her whenever I can. She's retired but pretty independent. Works part-time at a gift shop one street over from where she lives. Keeps her busy. And she crochets a mean baby blanket. Sends sets of hats and blankets to the Priory Hospital. If they have a surplus, they send them on to others."

"Siblings?"

"No, just me. I had a sister, Eva, but she died before she was a year old. I don't really remember her."

"I'm so sorry."

"Thanks. Me too. It would have been fun to have a

little sister to look after and protect."

Olivia came over to collect their plates; it looked like they were getting ready to close. "Can I get you anything else?"

Paisley looked at Finlay, then Olivia. "I'd love an order of blackberry crumble to go."

"Make that two," Finlay added, finger raised and smiling.

"Can you put it on my card, Olivia?"

"Sure thing, Sweet." Olivia paused. "So, it's back to Bonchurch tomorrow?"

"Yes, I'm afraid so. I have to get back to the real world and help my mum in the bookshop while matters at Thornberry get sorted out."

"Well, I hope they get sorted out soon so you can come back and see us."

"Me, too, Olivia. Me, too."

"How about dessert in front of a fire in the drawing room?" Paisley suggested on the ride back to Thornberry Manor. She looked over at him with a smile. "Think you can manage a fire?"

"Sounds perfect, and yes, I can manage a fire." He took her hand, gently squeezed it, and gave it a light kiss.

"And I think I can manage two spoons."

Finlay pulled up to the dark, hulking manor and

parked his truck in front of the door. "You should really leave a light on if you're not going to be back before dark. I know it's safe around here, but I'd feel better knowing you at least had some light to help you find your way." He led her to the front door and opened the flashlight app on his phone to help her find the keyhole.

He was so close and smelled of warm wool, the soap he'd used in the kitchen, and the impossible-to-describe essence of being male. She turned to thank him and received a warm, light kiss instead. "Sorry. I couldn't resist."

Paisley managed a smile, but no words could be coaxed from a tight throat that felt like it was full of cotton. Instead, she took his hand and kissed its rough, hard-working skin. "You're forgiven," she whispered. "You do the fire, and I'll get spoons."

They ate in relative silence, murmuring to themselves and each other how delicious it was, how it was made, and if there was a chance Olivia would give them the recipe. Finlay had tucked the chairs next to each other in front of the fire, and when he finished, set his to-go box on the floor and put his arm around her as best he could. "These chairs don't lend themselves very well to any degree of closeness. I have a better idea."

He added a hefty chunk of oak to the fire, took the cushions and arranged them on the floor, and invited her to join him. "Ah. Much better, don't you think?"

"Mmm. Much better." She settled in the crook of his arm and rested her head on his chest. "Perfect, in fact."

"Can perfection be improved upon? I think so." Without giving her a chance to answer, he leaned over and kissed her. Softly at first, then with more intensity and passion. He knew how to kiss. She wasn't sure how or where he learned, and she didn't care. They melded like they were made for each other.

She could have gone on kissing him forever and gone far beyond kissing. Finlay showed great restraint, which both disappointed and impressed her. He seemed determined not to rush things, even when his body was telling them both otherwise. After enveloping her in one last, lingering hug, he got up and prepared to leave. "If I don't go now, I won't be held responsible for what will happen."

Paisley got up and reluctantly put the chairs back in order. "Sometimes I wish you weren't so level-headed and gentlemanly."

"Me neither, but there it is." He pulled on his jacket and Paisley walked him to the door. "What time does your train leave?"

"Ten, I think."

"Well, then, I'll be here to collect you between 8:30 and nine. Will that give you enough time?"

The atmosphere shifted from intimate to formal. Back to real life. Business as usual. "Yes, that'll be fine." Paisley stifled a sigh as Finlay put on his shoes. She didn't want to appear pouty, but that's how she felt.

"Until the morning then." Finlay pulled her into his arms and kissed her again. Intense, thorough, and succinct. "Sleep well, Paisley. And lock the door behind me."

"I will. Goodnight, Finlay, and be safe." From the drawing room window, she watched the tail lights on his truck until he was out of sight. *Please be safe. I'm falling in love with you.*

16

Chapter Sixteen

There was time for a quick kiss and hello hug, then Paisley changed and helped her mum in the shop. It wasn't until after dinner that they had time to sit and catch up on each other's news.

"So, your research. Did you uncover anything interesting?"

"Nothing earth-shattering, and I'd have to get on the computer, which I don't feel like doing after a long day. How about we start with news from your end?"

Paisley sensed it was not a good time to reveal

anything about the necklace, so she focused on other things. "Well, the inspector and appraiser came; we should have their reports next week. And I hope to hear about our grant application soon." She shifted on the couch. "Finlay helped cover the roof in the conservatory, and I saved some of the glass pieces that had pattern on them. He thinks we can find someone who can duplicate them."

"Finlay sounds like a great help." Molly smiled and winked at Paisley.

"Oh, Mum. There you go, trying to find someone for me." She couldn't stop the blush she felt coloring her cheeks, so she ignored it and kept on talking. "He is really nice and so much help with Thornberry. He wants to see it restored as much as we do. And I got a lot of cleaning done, but you've already seen the photos and video about that."

"Did you bring that pretty necklace back with you?"

Paisley gulped. "I did. It's in my suitcase somewhere. How about we look at the ancestry stuff on Sunday, and I can show it to you then?" She'd promised her mum she'd tell her about it, but she was having second thoughts. She needed time to figure out *if* she was going to tell her mum—and if so, how.

"That will work out. I need your help with a book order tomorrow, and my brain will be mush after that. The promotion on 19th century female authors was a hit, so I need to place an order to replenish our stock."

Paisley's mind immediately rocketed to the copy of *Frankenstein* that Mary Shelley had given her, but she forced herself to focus on what her mum was saying and not risk suspicion or questions. "Sure. The books sold should be tallied on the register, so we can use that to make our replacement order."

"We should come up with a promotion for February, maybe something for Valentine's Day?"

"Sure. I can make a window display tomorrow and another book table inside. And I'll post something on our website. Love and romance, tragic or otherwise. I can do a combination of contemporary and historical authors of romance, like *A Summer of Secrets* and *Wuthering Heights*. We can call it something like Love and Romance Through the Ages."

"Oh, that sounds great! You always come up with such good ideas."

"I'll do a quick inventory of our romances in case we need to add to our order." She finished the glass of wine she'd started at dinner and rubbed her eyes. "I'm really bushed, Mum. I'm going to bed. We'll get the order and the promotion figured out tomorrow, okay?"

Molly got up and gave her a hug. "Thank you, Poppet. I knew I could count on you." She stepped back with a strained look on her face. "Sometimes this shop is more than I can handle."

"What about Alice? I'm sure she'd come and put in some hours with you if you need help."

"Oh, she would. But I like having you around. I like your ideas and the creative life you give to the shop. Neither of us can manage a website, let alone come up with the promotions you do that turn out to be so popular. And now you have the responsibility of Thornberry Manor on your shoulders."

Paisley gave her a warm, squeezy hug. "Don't worry about Thornberry, Mum. We have it well in hand at this point. And we'll figure out what to do going forward once we hear from the inspector and appraiser. Let's both get a good night's rest, and we'll deal with tomorrow when we get there. And Sunday we can relax and talk about Thornberry if you want. I'll make us a yummy treat, like bread pudding."

"Sounds perfect. See you in the morning."

"Goodnight, Mum." She sat on the bed and read a text from Finlay while she waited to use the bathroom.

Hi, Paisley! Hope you made it back safe and sound. Thanks for leaving the keys to Thornberry with me. I can swing by and check on things, and someone coming and going will deter those with mischief on their mind. We're getting a rain/snow mix just now, so I'll check on our roof patch tomorrow on my way back from transporting guests to Cliffe Castle Museum. I pick them up Sunday and bring them to the train station. I wish you could be there when I open the door, but I'll do my best in your absence.

Warm hugs,

Finlay xx

Paisley smiled and set the phone aside. She needed a long soak in the tub and didn't want to appear too eager with an immediate response to Finlay. She didn't know anything about his past relationships with women. Did it really matter? Perhaps it was better to let the past stay in the past. She laughed quietly, sputtering the hot water in front of her lips as she remembered where the necklace had taken her. The past, indeed.

She couldn't deny that it had happened. Was it a fluke, some accident or wavering in the fabric of the universe? It would probably never happen again, so there was no point in telling anyone. It would get out of hand very quickly, and she couldn't explain how or why it had happened. Best to keep it safe and hidden.

Curled under the covers, she pulled out her phone and answered Finlay's text.

Hi, Finlay! It's good to hear from you — thanks for watching over Thornberry while I'm away. I'm going to help Mum with a book order tomorrow and then make a promotional window/table display for Valentine's Day. I will let you know as soon as I hear from the inspector and appraiser. That may determine my next trip to Thornberry. Keep me posted on how things are going there.

Hugs back,

Paisley xx

Her last thoughts before falling asleep were about finding a jeweller (preferably in London, where no one knew her) to look at the necklace and see if the stone could be replaced. There weren't any markings on it other than the initial, but maybe the metal encasing the orb and the chain might provide a clue about its history or origin. It was worth a try. At any rate, it was a pretty necklace and a family heirloom worth saving and restoring.

Two questions loomed large: If she put the necklace on anyplace other than inside Thornberry Manor, would she be transported to the past or remain in the present? Was she brave enough to find out?

17

Chapter Seventeen

It was a few minutes backtracking from the Farrington tube stop in London to Bleeding Heart Yard where Theodore & Son Jeweller was located. There were jewellers in Bonchurch, to be sure, but Paisley wanted her dealings with the necklace kept as discreet and confidential as possible—at least until she had some idea of what she was dealing with. Gandalf's warning to Frodo in *The Fellowship of the Ring* played over and over in her mind. *Keep it secret. Keep it safe.*

She'd shown it to her mum on Sunday, as promised.

The stone crumbs were safely stored in a small, plastic container; her mum wondered aloud at the state of them as she gently shook it. "How could they break apart like that?"

"I'm not sure, but I'm going to ask the jeweller what kind of stone it is. That might explain something."

"Why are you taking the necklace all the way to London?"

"Well, I have some things to check on related to Thornberry. I want to stop in and see where the appraiser and inspector are with our reports. Sometimes it's good to show up in person to remind them there's a sense of urgency. On our part, anyway." Paisley grasped at something else that would justify the trip. "I figured I could find a jeweller there, and if I have time, I'll stop by a couple of bookshops to see how they look and what kind of displays they have." She smiled and winked at her mum. "Always good to see what the competition is up to, right?"

"I guess so. It just seems like a long trip for things you could get done here."

"Well, not all of them. And I'll be there and back in one day. It'll be a quick trip."

Paisley chose to travel to London on Tuesday to avoid the Monday rush for those who'd escaped the city over the weekend. The sun popped in and out between the clouds prodded along by a brisk, easterly breeze. She was glad for her wool coat and neck scarf as she made her way toward the two-storey, brick-faced façade. She wasn't sure why she'd chosen Theodore & Son; there were jewellers aplenty in the district, but something told her this might be a good fit.

The soft tinkling of a bell above the door announced her arrival as she opened the heavy, oak door. "Good morning, Ma'am." The grey-haired man smiled warmly at her as she walked up to the counter. "What can I help you with today?"

Paisley took the necklace from her purse and placed it on the counter between them. "I found this, and I wonder if you can tell me anything about it." She set the plastic container next to the necklace. "I'm pretty sure this is what's left of the stone that was in the setting. Can you tell by these bits what kind of stone it was?"

The man wore a dark, finely-tailored suit, expensive cologne, and on his left lapel was a name badge with the name Leo on it. "I'm fairly certain we can identify the stone type." He picked up the necklace and examined it; Paisley held her breath as she watched for any changes in his expression that would alert or alarm Leo, but his features remained passive and focused as he continued his inspection. "Are you wanting to replace the stone?"

"Yes, once we figure out the identity of the one

that's here in bits and pieces."

"Well, if you can leave it with us for a few days, we can do some investigating about its age and possible origin, and I can provide you with an estimate to replace the stone."

Paisley provided him with her contact information and took one of the business cards from the brass tray on the counter. "You will be careful with it, yes? You'll keep it safe?"

"Of course, Ma'am. Rest assured we will take the utmost care with your necklace." He reached across the counter and shook her hand. "Not to worry, Ma'am."

She was reluctant to leave the necklace, but there was no help for it. "Thank you. Take whatever time you need. I'm not in a huge rush for it, and I want to give you time to research it thoroughly and then talk about replacing the stone."

"Absolutely. Thank you for entrusting your treasured possession with us."

"You're welcome. Goodbye then."

"Good day, Ms. Venne."

Paisley found a bench in the sun and called the appraiser's and inspector's office. Neither Jack Hunter nor Mason Grant was available, but their assistants told her she'd have a copy of the report emailed to her by the end of the day. After she hung up, she sent a quick email to Andrew

Collins at Morgan and Butterfield and told him she'd forward the reports as soon as she received them. His assistant, Nancy Garberly, called her within minutes of her sending the email.

"Hi, Paisley? It's Nancy from Morgan and Butterfield. I just wanted to let you know that we received your email, and I will make sure Andrew sees it and contacts you if he has any questions going forward."

"Thank you, Nancy. This is all new to me, so I'm trying to make sure everyone knows what is happening."

"Absolutely. I understand. And we'll do our best to help you as the process unfolds."

"Thanks so much."

"Goodbye, Paisley."

Paisley tightened her scarf and set off toward the Farrington tube stop where she discovered a small bookshop she hadn't noticed earlier. It was cute and quaint, about the size of their own Page-Turner Books in Bonchurch. She stood in front of the shop, admiring the lettering on its red and gold sign, *Greville Street Books*.

Forty-five minutes later she emerged with two books about restoration of estates and gardens and some ideas for displays and promotions in the bookshop. She wouldn't copy them exactly but tailor them to their own location and its personality. She took photos of the book covers and sent them to Finlay in a text.

Hi! In London for the day, contacting people about Thornberry. Trying to convey a sense of urgency on my part. Appraiser and inspector's office say I will have reports by the end of the day. Fingers crossed!

Found these at a local bookshop I passed by. Might give us some help/ideas going forward. On my way home now. Take good care.

Hugs,

Paisley XO

She called her mum, telling her she was on her way home and asking if she needed anything.

"No, I think we're set. I hope you don't mind pizza for supper."

"Pizza is fine. I'm on the train just now, then the ferry, and then I'll be home."

"See you soon, Poppet."

Paisley did random searches on her phone while the train swooshed along on its way to the ferry station. When she came across one about the meaning of names, she scrolled until she found the name Eva—Finlay's sister who died before her first birthday. The meaning didn't seem to fit. The name Eva meant *life* or *living one*. She wondered what had claimed little Eva's life so soon. She wasn't sure Finlay knew, either. Sometimes babies just didn't survive. She didn't have the heart to bring the subject up again; instead, she said a silent prayer for her as she watched the blurry world outside the window of the train.

18

Chapter Eighteen

The inspection was pretty much what she expected. The wiring needed to be re-done and the plumbing given an intensive upgrade. Significant energy usage would be reduced if the windows and doors were either repaired or replaced. Then there was the matter of the conservatory roof and the general integrity of that structure itself.

Paisley didn't see any of them as insurmountable. She was confident that Finlay and the other contractors could bring Thornberry Manor into compliance and restore its former beauty. She wanted her dream for the manor house to come true; it could be transformed into a breathtaking vacation destination or a retreat/event venue. She could live on-site and travel to Bonchurch when her mum needed her.

Another stroke of good luck! The appraisal had squeaked in under the £325,000 threshold, so there would be no estate taxes due. Andrew Collins from Morgan and Butterfield would see that a copy of the appraisal was sent to the tax office in London and would send her a statement for his services. Her body tensed about the money due and payable, but it couldn't be helped. It was all about moving toward Thornberry's recovery and restoration. She'd find a way to get them paid; the bookshop was doing well enough, and she'd take on another job if she had to. She wasn't sure how she'd find enough hours in the day to work two jobs *and* restore Thornberry, but she was determined to find a way. For now, she pushed the thought of a second job to the dark, dusty, never-gonna-happen corner of her mind.

Paisley shared the news with her mum after supper that evening. When Molly frowned with concern at the inspector's recommendations, Paisley was quick to come to Thornberry's defence. "We knew it would need some help, Mum. Maybe the Historic England grant will come through; that would be a huge help."

"When will you hear from them?"

"Well, I just made the application in January, so I don't suppose for a month or two. I could call tomorrow and see where my application stands and when I might hear back."

"Well, until then, let's focus on the shop. Can you work on the Valentine's Day window and display tomorrow?"

"I will, Mum. I promise." As she cleared the dinner plates away, she remembered something she wanted to investigate on her next trip to Thornberry. "Did you come up with any fairly recent names on your ancestry search? I want to compare them to any stones in the Thornberry cemetery that might be a match."

"I did find some interesting bits. I can print them out for you so you have them on your next trip."

"Do you remember any offhand?"

"Someone named Flery or Flanon."

"Flemon? Could it be Flemon Hix?"

"Yes, I think that's his name. I think his wife's name was Polly. You'll probably see their names on the stones."

Paisley gulped. She'd met both of them in 1829, along with their daughter Phoebe and infant son Henry. Knelt at the family monument stone and read Flemon and Polly's dates with the sad addition of Phoebe, dead at 20 with her daughter Primrose. What about Henry? He must be buried there, too. She remembered looking at the stone, but the rain had interrupted her exploration. As soon as the thought of finding Henry crossed her mind, a warning swiftly followed. *Do not seek him. Not now. Not yet.*

"And I think there was a son," her mum continued.

Paisley quickly changed the subject. "Well, you can give me a printout, and I can compare it with the stones in the cemetery. Now, about the Valentine's display. I have some ideas."

* * *

She wanted to get the window display finished before the shop opened for the day. As she cleaned the alcove, she glanced at the calm water across the street. The water in the channel looked like it was breathing, the surface rising and falling as if in a deep slumber. The fishermen and ferry boats would be glad for a day like today—if it held. For Paisley, it was a welcome distraction from Thornberry and the necklace, but they were never too far from her thoughts.

The heart-shaped lights would be romantic, cheery, and inviting. A vase of silk roses and ribboned bunches of lavender were tucked among the copies of books Paisley chose for the display. She decided to display photos of the authors in heart-shaped frames beside their literary works.

She knew *Pride and Prejudice* was popular with readers as she set a few copies on an easel with Jane Austen's photo next to it. Paisley found a small narrative and printed it on card stock to place next to Jane's photo. The fact that she visited the Isle of Wight in 1813 might prove interesting to local fans of her work. *Wuthering Heights* by Emily Brontë was a dark, haunting tale, but she wanted a mix of plots and storylines. For poetry lovers, she chose *Best Poems of the Brontë Sisters*, also by Emily and some by more recent authors like Danielle Steel and Leonard Nimoy. Diana Gabaldon's *Outlander* series was popular, and she found several by Susanna Kearsley, like *The Winter Sea* and *A Desperate Fortune*.

She finished arranging the display and stepped outside to see what it would look like to passersby. The air was salty and crisp, reminding her that calm, benevolent days like today were a gift not to be taken lightly or for granted. As she looked up and down the street, she saw Noah walking toward the wharf and the fishing boat he worked on. She silently wished him and the others a safe journey as she ducked inside before he caught sight of her. She wanted nothing more to do with him, but didn't want him or any of the others to get injured, or worse.

Molly came down with a plate of scones and tea as Paisley began work on the display table inside the shop. "Thanks, Mum." She'd forgotten about breakfast in her eagerness and determination to help her mum and distance her emotions from Thornberry. She sipped and pointed at the display window. "Check it out—I think it looks pretty good."

"It's clever and catchy. Well done."

"What if we run a special sale on Valentine's Day? Like buy one, get one one-half off. Something like that. We could limit it to in-store purchases only."

"That's a great idea!"

"Okay, let's figure out the details today, I can post something on the web, and make a sign to put in the display window."

Traffic and sales seemed to pulsate like the water in the channel. Busy, then quiet. Repeat throughout the day as needed.

The mail arrived around three, but Paisley forced herself to not open the envelope from the Historic England Grant Office in London. *After supper* she told herself as she tucked it into the pocket of her smock. *Then we can relax and enjoy the good news.*

The letter teased at her sense of discipline; every time she reached or crouched, it would crinkle and poke at her, pestering her to open it. Paisley responded with daydreams of various rooms in Thornberry getting well-deserved makeovers. The kitchen, conservatory, study, bedrooms–

every room would receive what it needed to begin a new life as a travel destination.

The last customers of the day popped open their brollies against the heavy mist settling on the walkway and road in what looked like the first round of what would probably be an all-night rain event. Paisley waved goodbye as she locked the door and lowered the shade.

Supper was a buffet of leftovers, a weekly ritual of clearing the fridge before the next grocery order arrived. Spoonfuls and slices of this and that, along with the last of the apple cake. It had been a good traffic day in the shop, and customers were drawn in by the window display. She'd do a quick inventory tomorrow in case they needed to order more books before Valentine's Day, and the website was updated to showcase the promotion and special pricing on Feb. 14th. It was all well in hand.

She quickly cleared the dishes and put them next to the sink. "C'mon, Mum. Into the living room so I can open the letter."

"Oh, it's so exciting, Paisley! I can't wait to hear what they have to say. Just think of all the things we can do for Thornberry with the grant money."

Paisley sat down and smiled at her mum. "Drum roll?" She carefully (and dramatically) loosened the flap on the envelope, unfolded the letter, and cleared her throat before she began to read. In a fraction of a second her dreams were dashed, the words collecting and colliding like dust in her throat.

Dear Ms. Venne,

Thank you for contacting Historic England and applying for restoration funds relative to your property, Thornberry Manor.

We regret to inform you that your application for funding has been denied.

She didn't bother reading the rest; the letter slipped from her hand and fell to the floor as Paisley dissolved in tears.

19

Chapter Nineteen

Paisley slumped forward from her spot on the couch. It was all gone. Her dream of restoring Thornberry Manor, keeping it as a family legacy, and living on the property that had been in her family for generations. It was all gone with the stroke of a pen. Award letters took forever, but there seemed to be a fast track for rejection letters.

Her visit there in 1829 felt like a fading fantasy, and Paisley began to wonder if it had really happened. Was it a dream? A fantasy dream blown out of proportion?

She'd known disappointment in her life, but nothing

like the utter defeat flowing over her in waves at this moment. Molly scooted over and pulled her into a hug. "There now, Poppet. Perhaps it wasn't meant to be."

Paisley's heartbreak morphed into anger—not at her mum, but there was no one from the historic board within earshot. "How can you say that, Mum? How can you just give up? Thornberry Manor belongs to *you*!

"I know that, Paisley, but some things may be beyond our doing."

Paisley was devastated, but she hated admitting defeat. Letting someone else win without a fair fight. She picked up the letter and scanned the rest of what she hadn't read. "No, this isn't beyond our doing. It says right here that we can appeal the decision. That we need to call them and schedule a hearing where we can present our case for reconsideration." She carefully folded the letter and set it on the table in front of them. "I'm going to call Andrew Collins first thing in the morning and see what he recommends. Maybe he'll come with me."

"Do you think it will change anything?"

"Well, I'm not going to just accept what they whipped out on this piece of paper and chucked into the post. There's a lot at stake here. For us, anyway. We have to try, Mum. I'm going to try, and you may need to come along since the property is legally yours."

"Of course, I will—if you think it will help."

"I think it will, and the more people we can have to argue our case, the better. I'm going to ask Finlay if he'll attend, too." She hugged her mum and got up from the couch. "I'm off for a bath and then I'm going to get a hold of Finlay. See you in the morning."

The long soak soothed her nerves and calmed the stinging agitation that clung to her since she'd read the rejection letter. When she climbed into bed, she was in a better mental state to talk it over with Finlay. "Hi, Finlay. Got a minute to talk?"

"Hi, Sweet. I'm just home from work, so let me get inside." Paisley listened to the sound of the truck door closing, boots on gravel, and a door opening and closing. She wished she was there to welcome him home and slip into one of his warm, enfolding hugs. "Okay, jacket off, and I'm on the couch. What's up? You sound concerned about something."

"I am. Sorry for being so blunt, but it's about Thornberry." Paisley felt her throat tighten and the tears prickle at her eyes; this time, there was no stopping them. "They rejected the grant, Finlay. Historic England isn't going to give us any money." A string of silence stretched out between them as Paisley sobbed quietly and Finlay patiently waited, letting her emotions have the space they needed.

"You sound like you need a hug and lots of kisses."

"I do, but I need to ask a favor of you."

"Ask away."

"I decided I'm going to appeal the decision. I'll have to schedule a hearing and appear in London. Would you be willing to attend and speak up for Thornberry? You've been around it more than Mum or I, and you know what restoring it would mean as a historic property to the people who are supposed to be promoting and supporting that very thing. Visitors to the area would bring in business, and promoting Thornberry would mean promoting Keighley and the surrounding area. You have a unique perspective that neither Mum nor I have, and I think it might help."

"Of course, I will attend the hearing and lend whatever support I can. Just tell me when and where, and I'll be there."

"Well, I have to contact them first and request one. I'm going to ask Andrew Collins from the solicitor's office to be there as well."

"Don't give up, Paisley. So many of these things start with rejections. They figure if a certain percentage accept that, they're money ahead. We won't let that happen to Thornberry."

Paisley released the tense, tight air in her lungs she didn't realize she'd been holding. "I feel so much better after talking to you."

"We'll get it sorted right enough. Don't you worry."

"I hope so."

A pause on the line. "So, when is your next trip to Thornberry? That big, old house misses you, and so do I."

Paisley smiled. "Well, not as soon as I'd like. We have a promotion going for Valentine's Day, and I need to be here to help Mum. As soon as I can get away after that, I'll be up."

"Is there anything you need me to do, aside from the occasional visit to make sure it's safe and secure?"

"Not really. We can't do anything major until we hear about the grant. So, when I come up, it will just be more house cleaning and yard work. Maybe we can make a trip to the glass man and see what he has to say about the ceiling panels for the conservatory. If you can get some rough measurements, maybe he can give us an estimate. Do you think the framework is okay, or will that have to be rebuilt?"

"I'm not sure. When I go up for the measurements, I'll take another look at it."

Paisley shifted in bed and looked at the time. "I better let you go. You've probably had a busy day."

"Yes, it was, and I'm starving." Paisley heard what she thought was his refrigerator opening. "Let me know when you get a hearing date so I can make sure I'm free to attend."

"I will. I don't know how to thank you, Finlay."

"Oh, I could offer up a couple of ideas here and now, but I'll save them for when we're together at Thornberry."

"Fair enough, and now I'm curious."

"Well, that will have to hold you. Goodnight, Sweet."

"Hugs, Finlay. Hugs and kisses."

20

Chapter Twenty

A brisk, March breeze skittered past Paisley and her mum as they approached the entrance to the London office of Historic England. The imposing, multi-storey building looked conflicted with the sign that hung above the glass and metal doors. Nothing much historic to see here, it seemed to say.

Andrew Collins was seated on a wooden bench in the foyer and stood with a smile to greet them as they approached. "Good morning, ladies. I have a good feeling about the hearing today."

"I'm glad you do. I'm quite nervous about the entire thing," Molly said as she fussed with her tousled hair and straightened her jacket.

"It'll be fine, Mum. Positive vibes, okay?"

Andrew beckoned toward the long, stone staircase. "Let's head upstairs, shall we?"

They were halfway up when Paisley heard her name echo in the foyer below. It was Finlay, pulling on a tweed jacket and taking the stairs two at a time to catch up to them. It was all Paisley could do to stop herself from hugging Finlay; instead, she introduced him to Andrew Collins and smiled as he greeted Molly. "It's nice to see you again, Mrs. Venne. I'll do whatever I can to restore Thornberry Manor for you and your family."

"Thank you, Finlay. We appreciate the time and effort it took to help us today."

"Happy to help, Mrs. Venne." Finlay took Paisley's hand and gave it a quick, tender squeeze. A smile, a wink, and they were at the top of the stairs on their way to the hearing room.

Nearly three hours later (most of it spent waiting for their case to be called), they emerged feeling that they'd done their best to convince the board members to award them a grant. Paisley had provided them with an impressive portfolio reflecting the current state of Thornberry and what needed to be done to restore it. She included her vision for what the property could become, the benefits to the surrounding communities, and England in general as a destination for visitors interested in history and historic buildings.

Finlay was next and supported her presentation with a sincere, heartfelt explanation of his role in the effort to secure a historic grant for Thornberry. He had no notes but spoke eloquently, sincerely, and gently about his observations of its decline and that it was not too late to save the property. He believed his current profession qualified him to speak with authority on the issues that were critical and needed immediate attention along with those that could be solved with manual, free labor.

"When did you last visit the property?" one board member asked.

"I was there yesterday," Finlay replied. "I have photos on my phone if you'd like to see some of the areas I referenced." The board member nodded and extended his hand.

While the board members passed the phone back and forth, Andrew Collins spoke about the legal transaction and life event that led to them appearing at the hearing.

Lastly, they asked if Molly would like to speak on behalf of Thornberry Manor and what a restoration grant would mean to her. She had no prepared notes, either, and Paisley could only wonder what she was going to say. "I'm a bookshop owner from Bonchurch," she began. "I had no idea this property would pass to me until I received the letter from Mr. Collins." Paisley could tell she was nervous by the folding and unfolding of her hands, but she maintained her poise and focus. "Thornberry Manor is mine now and will someday belong to my daughter, Paisley. I do not have the expertise, nor the ability, financial or otherwise, to restore Thornberry and prepare her for her next role in life. For that, I need your help. We need your help."

Molly started to sit, then rose again. "We can send regular updates, photos, and whatever documentation you require to ensure we are spending your money wisely and to best effect." She turned and looked over her shoulder. "Paisley's quite good at sending things electronically." She paused as her emotions took hold. "For whatever reason, you decided we weren't worthy of a grant to restore Thornberry Manor. I am here today to tell you we are. I am. Worth the money I need to restore my family home and give it a new life. Thank you for your time—I hope you will help us."

The lone female on the board spoke up as they prepared to leave. "Thank you, all of you, for coming in today and showing us what Thornberry Manor means to you, the community, and England itself. We will review your appeal and submit a response before month's end." The other members looked at her in disbelief. "Yes, before month's end," she repeated. "These people have taken the time and trouble to come here and ask for what they need. The least we can do is show them the courtesy of a prompt review and response."

Andrew stood in the hall, grinning as he waited for the door to close behind them. "Well, I think we have at least one member on our side."

Molly sat on the wooden bench next to the railing, overwhelmed by what she had just done. "Do you think so, Andrew? Do you think we convinced enough of them?"

"I hope so, Molly. We gave it our best shot, and all of you did a great job of viewing the need from your individual perspective." He stretched out his arm and looked at his watch. "I need to get back, but I'll have Nancy on the alert for news from the board. If any of you hear, please share it around so we all know what is going on."

Heads nodded in agreement, goodbyes were exchanged, and Andrew hurried down the steps and out the door. Paisley looked at her phone. It was too late to visit Theodore & Son about the necklace; by the time she got there, they'd be closed. She'd call tomorrow and talk to Leo. The warning flashed again in her mind. *Keep it secret. Keep it safe.*

"We've got to be getting back, Finlay. We have a bit of a journey yet to go."

"I understand. I'll walk you out—I can do that much." He took both her and Molly's hands as they descended the staircase and gave Paisley's cheek a quick, discrete kiss before letting go. "Have a safe journey home. Please, let me know when you hear, and I'll do the same."

When they got outside, Molly gave Finlay a quick, appreciative hug. "Thank you, Finlay. We've come to depend on you so much; I hope you know how much it means to us. We don't want to take you for granted."

"I understand, Mrs. Venne. At some level, we're all in this together." His broad smile and bright, blue eyes displayed his genuine affection for her and Paisley. "Now, if you don't mind tucking together in the front seat of my truck, I'd be happy to deliver you to the train station. I can at least get you that far."

21

Chapter Twenty-One

The journey to Thornberry Manor was becoming more familiar and seemed shorter with every trip. She was on a first-name basis with some of the ferry attendants and train staff since she kept to the same timetable going back and forth. Knowing Finlay would be at the station to meet her filled her with warm, glad anticipation.

She was making the trip without the necklace. She'd called the jewellery shop and spoke to Leo the day after the March 15th hearing for an update. They were backed up with the usual Valentine's Day business and the re-sizings and alterations that came after, but the necklace was on his project list. He determined that the stone fragments were indeed pieces of an emerald. Old, to be sure. Did she want them back? Paisley wasn't sure why she'd need to keep them, but asked Leo to hold on to them for now. Could they be put back in the setting? They could, he'd responded, but it would be a more fragile setting than if she replaced it with a single stone. Did she want another emerald? Should he look for one for her? Paisley wasn't sure about that, either. "Can I think about it and let you know?"

"Absolutely. We'll keep it here and keep it safe until you decide what you want to do."

"What about the setting? Are there any markings or unusual metals in the setting or chain?"

"Nothing on first inspection, but I will look at it again. It appears to be an old silver compound, perhaps with some pewter. Do you want me to clean it?"

"I don't want it to be shiny and new-looking. Just a gentle cleaning, not a heavy polishing." She hesitated, but went ahead. "Do you have any idea of the age of the necklace or its origin?"

"I'm still looking into that. I have some ideas, but nothing certain. I've seen some pieces similar to yours, but nothing exactly like it."

"Thank you, Mr. ... Oh, my. I'm sorry," she

stammered. "I only know you by your first name from the badge you wear at the shop."

"It's more than acceptable. Feel free to call me Leo."

"Okay. Thanks, Leo. I'm curious to hear what you may find."

"Where did you get it, if I may ask? It may help me with my research."

Paisley tensed, but there was no harm in telling the truth. "I found it at a property my mother recently inherited. An old manor house near Keighley."

"That's an interesting detail, but probably has no bearing on the necklace itself. I will contact you if I find anything earth-shattering, and you can get back to me on the matter of the stone."

Speaking with Leo about the necklace and its mysterious origin restored in her the assertion that she had actually traveled back in time to 1829, although nothing in the necklace would probably reveal that to anyone. She hadn't dreamed or imagined it, and she felt safe believing it. For that, she was grateful. For now, her secret was safe.

The good news for Thornberry Manor arrived on the last day of March. Paisley was pretty sure the woman on the Historic England Board had been instrumental in approving their appeal for funding to restore and repair the beautiful, but neglected manor house. Paisley promptly wrote to the board, thanking them for reconsidering, assuring them that all of the criteria related to the grant would be adhered to, and regular updates would be shared with the board.

When the letter arrived in the mail, Paisley had been too nervous and handed the letter to her mum to open and read. She remembered pacing back and forth in their small living room, watching the ivory paper quiver in her mum's hands as she read aloud in a trembling, hesitant voice. Then they'd hugged and did a silly dance to celebrate the new life for Thornberry and for each other. Life would be forever changed going forward, and it would involve embracing change and inevitable doubts and challenges.

* * *

Paisley checked her phone after waking from a quick, Sunday afternoon nap on the train. Finlay had sent her a photo of the orange tree in the conservatory.

New leaves coming! I moved it to a sunny spot and will cover it if a cold night is forecast. It will need fertilizer soon. I'll pick some up.

I got takeaway for dinner. Fancy some hearty soup and

fresh rolls? Won't tell you what dessert is!

She secretly hoped it was blackberry crumble but was grateful for the dinner and whatever sweet treat would follow.

Thanks for getting dinner! Can't wait to see you! About 20 minutes.

Paisley XO

She hurried off the train, running as her bag zig-zagged behind her from one wheel to the other and her backpack bounced against her back. She let the handle go as Finlay scooped her into his arms. "Oh, Sweet, it's been too long," he whispered before kissing her without concern for anyone who might be watching.

"You're right about that," Paisley answered when she'd caught her breath. He held her hand the entire trip to Thornberry; they ate lukewarm soup in front of the fire in the drawing room and apple cake in bed after they'd made love. It wasn't something either of them had intended, but it happened, and Paisley was glad for it. Finlay was tender and passionate, considerate and intuitive. She smiled at the last descriptive terms floating through her mind; it sounded a bit clinical and un-romantic, but he instinctively knew how to please her without her fully realizing it herself. Finlay being intuitive and instinctive was perfect in her mind.

She nestled next to him as he put his arm around her and pulled her close. The soft hair on his chest was a warm, furry pillow that lulled Paisley to sleep as she listened to the sound of his strong, steady heartbeat. Toward morning, she'd happily welcomed him again; this time it was slow and gentle, like easing into the new day. He laughed as they untangled limbs and covers afterward. "If we don't get up and do something, we're likely to be at it all day. I'm not sure that I have enough stamina, but I'd gladly give it a try."

Paisley giggled and patted his firm, softly-fuzzed butt. "As much as I'd like to take you up on your offer, my bits could use some recovery time."

"So, what's the plan for today?"

"Well, we could take photos of the conservatory framework and then figure out how much can be saved and what needs to be replaced. Then maybe a trip to the glass man?"

"How long can you stay this trip?"

"I'll go back next Sunday."

"Then we have one, full week together. Plenty of time to get Thornberry started." Finlay stretched and climbed out of bed. "How about we start at Paul's Glass?

He's the guy I took the conservatory pieces to. He can give us an idea for the cost to replace them and advise us on the framework. By the time we get back, it will be warm enough to work outside if you want."

"Sounds perfect. How about tea and a bagel for the road? I brought some up with me, and there should be some butter and jam in the refrigerator."

As they left Thornberry in Finlay's truck, Paisley suggested they contact an electrician and plumber to provide estimates. "I have copies of the inspection reports with me, so let's try and set up a time to meet with them while I'm here. If they could come the same day, that would be even better. That would free us up for the other days."

She glanced out the window at the dormant, rolling landscape, and an idea popped up. "Maybe we can look at the upstairs and see if there's a way to get another bedroom or two and another bathroom up there. We need to make good use of the space if we're going to have paying guests here. One or two choices won't be enough."

"I agree. The best time to do it is now if we're going to be opening up walls and installing new wire and pipes. So, I'll try and get the guys for Wednesday; that way, we'll have tomorrow to come up with some ideas."

"We should probably think about outdoor lighting. Even if we don't do it right away, maybe the electrician can put in a big enough service to add something later."

"Good thinking, Sweet." Finlay took her hand and kissed it as they turned the corner and pulled up in front of Paul's Glass.

Paisley stopped in the driveway as a cloud of concern floated over her face. "I need to read through the grant paperwork again to be sure what we can and can't do. I want to make sure I don't get carried away and end up having to pay for something they would have covered."

"We can go through it tonight—together and make sure we stay within their criteria. How does that sound?"

"Sounds like a plan."

Finlay leaned down and gave her a quick kiss as he opened the door. "Homework first, fun later."

22

Chapter Twenty-Two

Finlay was called away to work on Tuesday at the Silent Inn, and Paisley secretly welcomed a day of solitude at Thornberry. As much as she cared about Finlay, she needed some quiet, reflective time to wander around the house and get to know it on a more personal level, like reuniting with a long-lost relative.

She found a sunny, sheltered spot outside the entrance to the conservatory and gently wrestled the orange tree next to the stone wall. Once they started work on the roof, the other plants would have to be moved outdoors; for now, they were protected from a sudden chill or overnight frost. She could cover it or bring it back inside before she returned home to Bonchurch, but the sprouting leaves made Paisley want to let it bask in whatever warmth the pale, April sun was able to muster.

She gathered the smaller pots together in small groupings and swept the flagstone floor, working under the plastic covering overhead that rose and settled with the air currents as if it were alive and breathing. Thornberry Manor was beginning a new life.

They'd stopped at a grocery store on the way home from Paul's Glass yesterday, so there was more than butter and jam in the refrigerator. At least, there were choices and ingredients to work with. Paisley assembled a roast with potatoes, carrots, and onions and put it in the oven for a long, slow bake. Then a grilled cheese sandwich for herself which she decided to savor in the study along with fresh, green grapes and iced tea.

The light was perfect in the study this time of day. The windows faced south/southeast and filled the room with light when the heavy drapes were pulled aside. Paisley wandered around the room while she ate, studying the layout of the room and moving furniture around in her mind. *I should get that software that interior designers use. Maybe not. Sometimes a tape measure is enough.* The furniture looked structurally sound with interesting, carved details; perhaps a good cleaning or reupholstering would be all that it needed. She reminded herself to ask Finlay about an upholsterer. Projects like that would be further down the road, but it wouldn't hurt to check into what was available and how much it would cost. She wasn't sure the Historic England grant would include something like reupholstering furniture—they might have to cover those costs on their own. She could always ask, and that kind of research was a pleasant diversion from the drudgery of electricity and plumbing.

This could be a pleasant room for visitors to gather. A table or two and some chairs could be added for card-playing or board games. The furniture would be arranged to create conversation groups, and there were plenty of books to read. Paisley leaned back on the couch and studied the shelves. They were old books, to be sure. She could order a sampling of current titles along with some books about the history and geography of the area where Thornberry was located. Some people would find that interesting.

If there were any rare or valuable volumes, Paisley felt they should be removed for safekeeping. Or maybe install glass doors with a lock to protect them? Better to see what she was dealing with first; it would be a good project for the rest of the day. She found a couple of empty boxes in the kitchen, dusting cloths and cleaner, and set to work on the first set of shelves.

She should have known that it was not going to be a quick, easy task for a lover of books. The books were old, perhaps of significant value. Paisley wondered if they were original to the house and the collection added to over the years. There was a set of 23 encyclopedias with gold lettering on dark, burgundy leather. The first volume had a publication date of 1854.

The sun transformed the floating dust motes into glittering, diamond flecks as she cleaned the shelf, wiped down each volume, and returned them to their original resting place. She made a concerted effort not to inspect every volume on the rest of the shelf; there would be plenty of time to savor them later. For now, a cleaning and general inventory was the order of the day.

Paisley did a pretty good job of adhering to her self-imposed, clean-and-move-on strategy until she reached the middle of the second set of shelves. There, she discovered a treasure trove of books by authors that included Charles Dickens, Charlotte and Emily Brontë, and Sir Walter Scott. She gasped when she opened some of the covers and found them autographed by the author. How had the books come to rest on Thornberry's shelves? Had the book been purchased or gifted to one of her ancestors? Had any of these authors been a guest at Thornberry? Many of them would have been contemporaries of past generations of her family. Paisley typed the names into the notes app on her phone so she could compare them to the members of her family living at the same time. Her mum most likely had some matches in her ancestry database already and would be willing to work on it for her.

After a quick bathroom break and a check on supper, Paisley returned to finish the last shelf in the study. It was after three, and Paisley wanted to finish the bookshelf task. The boxes she'd brought from the kitchen were still empty; she couldn't bear to part with any of the books on the shelves. Somehow, she'd find the money to have protective doors made and installed to keep them safe and secure.

In her haste to finish, she almost missed it—a dark, leather-bound book with simple lettering on the spine. The title *Frankenstein* was centered, and at the lower edge was the name of the author—*Shelley*. Paisley's hand trembled as she reached for the book. It was the same size as the one she'd clutched to her chest and tried to take back with her when she returned from the year 1829 to the present. But the book hadn't survived the trip; she'd arrived empty-handed.

The air in her lungs wouldn't move; it was as if they were waiting with her, suspended in anticipation. Paisley

THORNBERRY MANOR: THE EMERALD

opened the book to the title page. There it was, written in black, purposeful ink. *For Paisley.* Under her name was the signature of the author, *Mary Shelley*, and the year 1829.

23

Chapter Twenty-Three

Paisley gasped and began to sob. Loudly and uncontrolled, thankful that she was alone in the house. She wasn't sure why as she clutched the book to her chest, just as she'd done when she'd tried to take it with her when she left the year 1829 and returned to the present.

Someone must have found the book in her room and put it on the shelf. Hettie, her maid? Most likely. She wouldn't have thought anything of it as she was tidying up Paisley's room. The note she left behind would explain her abrupt departure, and that would have been the end of it.

The tears were a validation of all the doubt and uncertainty she'd been feeling; that somehow, she'd imagined or dreamt that it had happened. She wasn't sure how or why, but perhaps those answers would present themselves at some point. For now, she held the physical, tangible proof in her hands.

She stared at the dedication and signature, reliving the encounter in her memory until the sound of tires on gravel wrenched her from her interaction with Mary Shelley. It was probably Finlay. Panicked, she quickly tucked the book in a spot she'd remember—left set of shelves, second shelf from the bottom, fourth book from the left.

Finlay's predictable three-knock on the door told her it was him. He opened the door and called her name.

"In here, Finlay. In the study." Paisley backed away from the bookshelves and greeted him with a kiss when he came into the room.

"Hi, Sweet." He hugged her, then held her at arm's length and looked at her face. "What is it? What's wrong? You've been crying."

Paisley dismissed it with a wave of her hand. "Probably too much dust and cleaners. Which reminds me, I'd like to put some glass-fronted doors on these bookshelves and have locks installed on them. I looked at a few of the books, and they're quite old. We can display them, and I can order some books through the shop to have on hand for visitors to read if they want."

"Fair enough." Finlay moved to inspect the bookcases, and Paisley followed close behind, trying to ensure he focused on the structure of the shelves rather than the treasures they held. One in particular. Her chest tightened when he randomly pulled several volumes from the shelves. "There are some wonderful books here. I can see why you'd want to protect them."

"I do." She stepped back from the shelves as if to study them from a distance and pulled Finlay back with her. "I suppose you'll need the shelves emptied when you install the doors."

"Yes, to keep them safe and out of the way while we work."

The warning rose up and played again in her mind. *Keep it secret. Keep it safe.* "Well, we have other things to deal with before bookshelf doors, but I wanted to see if it was a possibility."

"Absolutely. When the time comes." He put his arm around her as they left the study. "Whatever it is that you're cooking smells delicious. How about we check it out and see about the rest of the evening?"

After dinner, they ventured outside through the conservatory. Paisley stopped in front of the orange tree as it proudly displayed its new, tender leaves. "It will be safe enough outside, don't you think? I mean, no frost or chill to damage it."

"It should be fine. It's mid-April, so we should be past the chance of any frost that might damage it. And you've got it in a sheltered spot, warm and protected with full sun during the day." Finlay reached down and patted the still-damp soil. "I fed it last week. With any luck, we might have blossoms and oranges this year."

"When will we know?"

"Well, according to what I read, they bloom sometime in May, and sometime around Christmas we should see fruit—green, with a potential hint of ripening."

"She's such a pretty tree."

"How do you know it's a *she*?"

"Because she has the potential to bear fruit. And I named her Shelley." As soon as the name passed her lips, she chastised herself for saying it. But there had been no forethought; the name just came out. If he didn't question it, no harm done. She breathed easier when Finlay shook his head and laughed.

"Should we walk up to the cemetery? The gate is a bit saggy, but I'm sure you can fix that easily enough."

Finlay took her hand as they walked the flagstone pathway leading to the walled-in, random arrangement of stones. "Yes, I can fix this gate," Finlay said as he swung it gently back and forth and studied it. "The posts have sunk over the years, but we can pull them up, put in some fill, and re-align them. Time, but not much expense."

Paisley purposely turned left when they entered the cemetery; she wanted to avoid the monument of Flemon Hix and his family, the family she visited in 1829. It was too sad for her to face just now. Phoebe and Primrose gone too soon. What about Henry? She knew he was dead, but didn't want to know and couldn't bear to look. Sometimes, she could almost feel that precious infant in her arms.

"Are we looking for anyone in particular? Or just looking?"

"Just looking for now. My mum has been researching our ancestry, and I thought I'd send her some photos of the stones of some family members. Maybe she can match them up with what she's found." The graves hugging the stone walls held the remains of ancestors older than those she had met, and she hoped her mum would have found them in their family tree. From the 1700s she found more Hix ancestors; the last name was spelled differently then. There was William and Prudence and Cornelius and Pearl. Roughly calculating the dates on the stones, Paisley guessed that William might be the son of Cornelius and Pearl; census and birth/death records on the ancestry site

160

would be able to establish their relationship. She took photos of those with her phone.

The cemetery itself was overgrown with grass and weeds, and ivy clung to the grey, stone walls. Even a few, small saplings had sprung up, taking advantage of the neglect to sprout and take hold. She'd make sure they were moved to a spot where they could flourish and thrive; there was no need to kill them just because they'd started their lives in the confines of a resting place designated for humans who had passed from this life.

"What about this family?" Finlay was standing in front of the monument Paisley was trying to avoid. "There's a bunch of people here."

Paisley felt her chest tighten. "I know. I already documented that one." She moved along the wall and stood at the gate. "C'mon, Finlay. Let's go."

He brushed away the grass obscuring Henry's name. "Must be the parents, a daughter Phoebe, a baby Primrose, and a son Henry." He knelt in front of the stone, calculating dates in his head. "Wow. Phoebe died young, and her baby... there's quite a story here." Flattening the grass, he looked at the opposite side of the stone. "Then we have Henry here. All on his own. Died in..."

Paisley turned her back to him and covered her ears. "Lalalalalalala...Stop! Don't say the date. Don't say it."

"Why? What's so important about him?"

"Nothing. He's not important."

"I don't understand. I thought you wanted names and dates for your research."

Paisley wrestled with the stubborn gate and sprinted down the hill toward the house. "Please don't ask, Finlay," she called over her shoulder. "And don't tell me!"

24

Chapter Twenty-Four

Paisley was watering the orange tree when Finlay came around the corner. One of the many things she loved about Finlay was that he was direct and honest. Trouble was, it wasn't a trait he turned on and off like a light switch. He was consistent, dependable, and predictable. Qualities she loved, just not right now. He came and stood next to her, but said nothing. It was her move.

"I'm sorry, Finlay."

"I don't understand. I was just trying to help."

"I know you were."

"Then tell me what's going on."

Paisley brought the watering can inside and set it down next to the sink. "I can't. At least, not now." She wanted to tell him, but the warning bells were clanging in her head along with that persistent message. *Keep it secret. Keep it safe.* "Please. You have to trust me on this."

"On what? I have no idea what you're talking about."

Paisley had to come up with a plausible explanation. Fast. "Let's just leave the cemetery out of our restoration equation for now. Mum and I are working on the ancestry part, and some of it becomes kind of personal, you know? So, if you can fix the gate, I'll deal with what's inside. How's that?"

"What about the mowing and moving those small trees?"

"I can do it. If I need your help, I'll ask."

Finlay's expression told her he wasn't completely sold on her explanation or request when he stepped away with his hands up in front of his chest. "I respect your need for privacy, but I can't abide secrets between us. They become a festering infection, a poison that destroys relationships." His dark, blue eyes looked sad and troubled as he put on his hat and gave her a kiss. "I'll be back tomorrow to help Scott with the electricity. He'll probably start at the panel box and go from there; you can let him know what rooms you want him to start with."

"Wait! You're leaving?"

Finlay turned back halfway to his truck. "I think we're both tired and need a bit of breathing room. I have some things to take care of for Olivia in the morning, then I'll be over to help Scott. Good night, Paisley."

"Good night, Finlay. Sorry." She was pretty sure he hadn't heard her as he climbed into his truck and drove away, but she was grateful that he couldn't see the tears that filled her eyes and spilled down her cheeks.

"What was I supposed to do?" she asked herself as she shut the door behind her. "Oh, by the way, I was in the year 1829 the other day. In this house. With my ancestors that are buried up in the cemetery. Other than that, nothing special." She continued the conversation as she marched up the stairs. It felt good to say it aloud to the empty house. At least she wasn't holding it in.

After a soak in the tub, she sent the photos she'd taken in the cemetery to her mum. *See if you can match these up with anyone you've found on the ancestry site.* Then she called because she needed to hear her voice.

"Hi, Mum. How are you? Everything going okay at the shop?"

"Yes, everything's fine. I just finished placing an

order to replenish the shelves. Alice has been helping me with a few things, and the weather has been good for people to be out and about."

"Well, I'll be home Sunday. Tomorrow the electrician is coming to get started on some things. Probably the basic service and then go from there. We'll see how far he gets and what he recommends."

"Will Finlay be there to help? We should probably start paying him for all that he's doing."

"He has some things to do for Olivia, then he'll be here. And yes, I'll ask him about payment. Now that we have the grant money, it's only fair to pay him." So, it would be back to a business relationship. "We owe him that much."

There was a pause on the line, and Paisley was pretty sure what was coming. "Is everything okay, Poppet? You sound like something's bothering you."

"No, Mum. I'm fine. Just tired, that's all." Her throat started to tighten, and she knew she had to hang up before the next wave of tears gave it all away. "How about I call you tomorrow, and I can send you some photos of what's happening? Scott will be here around eight."

"Perfect. I've got a haircut at eight, then I'll be at the shop."

They said their goodbyes, and Paisley sank down under the covers after setting the alarm on her phone. There would be no back-and-forth texting with Finlay. Her phone sat on the bedside table, black and silent. Paisley felt hollow and empty but refused to descend into the deep, dark depths of despair. Instead, she forced her focus onto Thornberry itself, her mother's manor house that held such promise, and vowed to do all that she could to bring it back to whatever life the future held.

What else could she do to take her mind off Finlay and what had happened between them? Well, she would update the spreadsheets she'd created to document her spending of the grant money, and she'd check with Nancy to see how often they wanted reports. She wished she had a computer and printer at Thornberry, but there was no cable extending the service to the house. She made a mental note to be sure Scott put that in the wiring plan; a desk could be set up in the study for guests who needed access during their stay. He would know what Internet providers were close enough to access their services. Until then, she could update her notes and send everything electronically when she returned home.

The roses needed pruning, but Paisley wasn't sure how to do it without damaging them. Her mum would know; she'd call, put a branch on the screen of her phone, and have Mum tell her where to cut. Then she'd apply the lesson to the abundant plantings around the exterior of

167

Thornberry and those in the conservatory waiting to be set outside. She was sure she could find what she was looking for on the Internet, but asking her mum would make her feel included and part of what was happening.

It would be a good task to work on while Scott and Finlay worked on the electricity. She'd be around to answer questions, but out of the way and distanced from Finlay. She was pretty good at reading moods and body language, so she'd observe Finlay when he showed up tomorrow; that would give her some indication of where things stood between them. She willed herself to believe that one disagreement wouldn't spell the end of their relationship.

Then there was the matter of the necklace. Tomorrow, she'd call Theodore & Son and see if Leo had learned anything about it. She'd come close to telling Finlay what had happened, but after this evening's uncertainty, she was glad she'd kept her secret safe. Anyway, the fact that the emerald was now little more than a thimble-full of deep, green crumbs was probably a good indicator that nothing like that would ever happen again.

25

Chapter Twenty-Five

Paisley was up, brewed coffee in hand, and had the rose tutorial done with Mum by the time Scott's van pulled up in front of the house. An early morning fog hung over the lake and hovered above the grass, but it would be gone as soon as the sun arrived and shooed it away. Paisley inserted the scene she loved from *Pride and Prejudice* into her mind, but there was no Mr. Darcy striding through the mist and tall grass to profess his love for her.

She took a sip of coffee and held out her hand to greet him. "Hi, Scott. I'm Paisley. Nice to meet you, and thank you for taking this on." His eyes were a paler shade of blue than Finlay's, and his hair the color of a weathered, rusty nail exposed to the elements for years. Shorter than Finlay, he had a stocky, strong build that Paisley felt when she shook his hand.

"Coffee?"

"Thanks, but no. I had mine on the way over."

"Right. Where would you like to start, then?"

"Well, I think at the panel, outside and inside. I need to see how big the service is and if we need to add to the amount of power coming into the house. From there, we'll feed what we need into the panel. It's near the kitchen, right?"

"Right."

"So, you might be without power for a while today, but I'll get that part done as quickly as I can."

Paisley pointed to the rose bushes clinging to the façade, framing the windows as they inched their way around them. "That's my project for today. Those and the others around here, so I won't need electricity for most of the day. Just a ladder and muscle power."

"You're not going to take them all the way down, are you?"

"Oh, no. Just pruning, removing the dead branches, and those that are heading in the wrong direction."

She took another sip of coffee, then pointed her finger in the air when she remembered what she wanted to ask him. "I'm not sure if any cabling for Internet needs to be added to your list. Can we take a look at what you have before you get started? Since we're basically starting from scratch, I'm trying not to forget anything."

"I understand completely. Let's go into the kitchen, and I can show you what I've mapped out."

Scott was thorough and forward-thinking. He'd anticipated and implemented the code changes and suggested several modifications to the kitchen and bathrooms that would make them more efficient and functional. Paisley showed him her ideas for the changes to the first floor where the bedrooms were and the additions that were still in the idea stage. "We'll need to get those walls changed and roughed in if that's what you want."

"I'm pretty sure, but I need to talk it over with my mum first. We still have some time before that needs to be decided, right?"

"Some, but not a lot. I need to know how large of a service to bring into the main panel and then into the house."

"And I need to show my plans to the board to see if they'll cover the expense."

Scott rolled up his electrical plan. "Well, there's

171

plenty I can do inside before we know the status of your additions, but I'd get it to them as soon as you can. You never know how long they will take to look at it and make a decision."

"Well, I already told them about my plans for Thornberry, so they shouldn't be surprised at the notion of adding two extra bedrooms and a bath. It was in the proposal we submitted, but I'll contact them, just to be sure."

"I'll leave you to your pruning, then. If you need electricity at some point, give me a holler, and I'll let you know where I am with all of it."

"Sounds like a plan. Thanks, Scott." Paisley stopped at the bottom of the kitchen stairs. "Finlay said he had a few things to do for Olivia and then he'd be over. I'll be outside with my pruners." She grabbed a day-old scone and motioned to Scott. "You're welcome to them, but they're not bakery fresh."

Scott looked over and laughed. "Thanks. I'm good for now."

Pruning the roses was a satisfying task now that she knew what to do. It had a peaceful, mindless quality to it. Sure, it was important to prune them properly, but once she had the technique down, it was just a matter of shaping and taming. Looking at the emerging leaves, she couldn't wait until they put forth buds and bloomed. It would be beautiful with some color and scent against the rough, grey stone. She'd text some photos to her mum later and ask her what kind of food she should give them.

Halfway up the ladder, she saw the dust curl on the road beyond the lake, and her breath caught in her throat. It was Finlay's brown truck. Chest tight, her heart pounded as she forced herself to finish the last, few cuts before climbing back down. What would it be like between them?

She stood next to the ladder as he pulled up and got out. "Hi, Finlay."

Without a word, he strode forward and pulled her into his arms. "I'm sorry, Paisley. I'm sorry for yesterday. I'm sorry for my impatience." He held her so close she could feel the beating of his heart. It reminded her of a quote she'd seen on a social media site—the beating heart and something about feeling so calm and safe that nothing could hurt you.

Paisley wished they could have stayed there forever, just as they were at that moment in time. "I'm sorry, too," she whispered. "Do you forgive me?"

He smiled at her, his blue eyes warm and endearing. "Say no more. Already forgiven."

Paisley shook her head and tried to explain, but ended up stammering and stumbling over her words. She was ready to confide in Finlay, but the words wouldn't come.

"It's just that… I don't know how…You'd never…"

Finlay interrupted her with a warm, thorough kiss and another hug. "When the time is right, you'll find the words." He smiled again and gestured toward the door. "How about we venture inside and see how Scott is doing?"

26

Chapter Twenty-Six

The goodbyes at the train station were becoming more painful and heart-wrenching. While the days at Thornberry scurried past, time crawled like a chilled, cold-blooded reptile until the next visit. How was it ever going to work out between her and Finlay? Long-distance relationships were challenging at best; she'd never had one, but that's what she'd heard and what the experts said. Would she move full-time to Thornberry? What about her mum and the bookshop?

As the train sped along, she felt like she was being

pulled in two directions at once with no solution to either one. Maybe if she didn't ruminate on it, the solution would present itself. For now, she'd focus on the restoration, helping her mum in the shop, and dealing with the necklace. And the ancestry stuff. That was more than enough to keep her busy.

She felt good about the electrical progress, and Frank had come out to look at the plumbing. The historic board had received their initial inspections and recommendations, and payment would be made as each phase was completed. Paisley felt good about that for a couple of reasons. One was that the contractors would be paid on time for the work they completed, and the other was that she didn't have to personally administer the funds. They'd be deposited electronically after approval by the fiscal member of the board, so she'd be kept out of any disputes about money or payment. Both Scott and Frank had her contact information, and Finlay would ensure they had access to the house when it was on their work schedule.

She leaned against the window, elbow on the sill, chin in hand. Finlay. Yes, she felt herself falling in love with him, and it thrilled and scared her. Her resolve not to dwell on him was failing miserably, so she gave in for the rest of the train ride and relived events in their relationship in no particular order, randomly plucking them from her memory like gathering a bouquet of wildflowers on a sunny, hilltop meadow.

When she was on the ferry, Paisley texted her mum and asked if she needed her to pick up anything on the way home.

No, Poppet. Just come home. Dinner is in the oven and brownies for dessert. XO

Molly popped the last bite of brownie into her mouth, wiped her fingers on a napkin, and turned on her laptop. "Look. I created this document that combines what I've found on the ancestry site with the photos you sent me." She patted the spot next to her on the couch. "Come and see. I found some photos on the site, too." Molly scrolled proudly through the screens as they perused them. "I can set it up like a book; when we're done, we'll have a wonderful history of my side of the family at Thornberry."

Paisley purposely bowed her head as if she was listening when Molly displayed the screen about Henry, then looked back as Molly moved on to other family members. What was it about him that affected her so strongly? She was grateful her mum hadn't announced the date of his death. If she had, Paisley would have had to cover her ears to block the news. Why? He was dead, like the rest of them, but something in her was attached to that tiny infant she'd held in her arms in the year 1829.

"Did you photograph all of the stones in the cemetery?"

"I think so, but I'll check them all again when I go back. It won't take that long." Paisley shifted on the couch. "I need to make a trip to London next week to check on my necklace, so let me know if there's anything you need or want while I'm there."

"I can't think of anything offhand, but ask me again before you go." Molly took a sip of her tea. "About the necklace," she started. "You said you were going to explain something about it when you came home. What was it you were going to tell me?"

The alarm bell in Paisley's head clanged non-stop as if some outside force was ringing a large brass bell outside a fire station. Following on its heels like wisps of smoke came the now-familiar warning: *Keep it secret. Keep it safe.*

"Oh, I was just going to fill you in on what Leo, the jeweller said. He didn't know much about it but was going to do some research since it's probably old. He wasn't sure what the stone was—he thought an emerald and probably knows for sure by now. The stone is damaged, so I'll have it replaced at some point. For now, I want to see what he

178

knows and the replacement cost. That's about it."

That was far from *it*. Paisley hated hiding things from her mum, especially something as otherworldly and bizarre as this. She justified it by the fact that she wasn't really lying, just holding back part of the story, albeit a major part. If Leo had any new information about the necklace, she'd share that, depending on what it was. She was pretty sure he wouldn't discover its ability to transport her through time.

As for the stone that had started out intact but ended up as crumbs, she didn't really have to address that. She told her mum the stone was damaged, and no more needed to be said about it if she decided to replace the stone. Why not? It was a beautiful necklace, had a beautiful, scrolly 'P' on one side, and with the stone replaced would most likely not pose any more time-traveling episodes. She wasn't sure where it came from or who it once belonged to, but that really didn't matter anymore. Unless some major bit of information came to light, she would keep and wear it as it was intended—a beautiful, family heirloom.

"So, what's happening in the shop that you need help with?"

"Well, Mother's Day is next month, so we should get some displays ready. Pregnancy books, new mom books, and probably children's books. I'm sure we have some props, and maybe when you go to London, you'll pass by that bookshop and see what they've got. Not that we'll copy them, but fresh ideas never hurt."

"I can do an inventory tomorrow, and then we can decide if we need to place an order."

Molly smiled and looked at Paisley with a mischievous wink. "And how is Finlay?"

27

Chapter Twenty-Seven

"Good morning, Leo." Paisley was happy to see him behind the counter at Theodore & Son but wasn't sure if he remembered her, so she introduced herself again. "I brought a necklace in to be repaired."

"Yes, I remember. You brought in a beautiful, old necklace with the broken emerald. I have it in the back— one moment."

Paisley's heart was glad to see it again. She smiled as Leo set it on a blue, rectangular pad in front of her. He'd cleaned it, but not polished, as she'd asked. "It looks so much better." Paisley picked it up and examined it. "Is the chain still sturdy enough? I wouldn't want to lose it because the chain broke somewhere and I didn't notice until it was too late."

"I checked the links and the clasp. Surprisingly, they're still in very good condition. Whoever owned this took very good care of it, or it wasn't worn very often."

"Were you able to find out anything about it? Like its age or where it was made? Anything like that?"

Leo reached under the counter and opened a manila folder, turning it so Paisley could see what was inside. "I researched some historic designs, and this is as close as I can come to the one you own."

Paisley studied the illustrations, then looked at Leo in wide-eyed disbelief. "Of course, there's no way to be sure, since there is no date or maker's mark on it. But I'm fairly certain this was made in the 18th century or earlier."

"Was it made here, in England?"

"Most likely. Perhaps right here in London." Leo pointed at the necklace. "The metal is somewhat of a puzzle. I'm fairly certain there is some silver and perhaps pewter based on its reaction to my cleaning it. But I think there's something else there, and I don't know what it is. I could send it off to a metal expert for testing and evaluation."

Paisley's protective instinct kicked in. She didn't

want the necklace subjected to harsh chemicals or whatever else might be involved, and part of her was afraid of what might be discovered. "No, I don't think I want to do that. I'm satisfied with what you've shown me."

"Fair enough. Well then, the next step will be to replace the stone if that's what you'd like to do."

"I'd like to, but I'm not sure with what. I guess it depends on what will hold up in the setting and the cost." Paisley looked at the tiny, oval cavity. The metal edges and framework felt warm to the touch but not to an alarming degree.

"Another emerald?"

If the emerald was the driving force behind her time-travel, Paisley was torn between choosing another emerald or something else. Still, one emerald was not the same as another, and the original was now a cluster of crumbs she'd saved in a small, plastic container. "Not necessarily. Anything in particular you'd recommend? For durability and stability, I mean. I think almost any stone would be beautiful in this setting."

"I can show you some replacement options and a general price point." Leo pulled out a laminated folder that was full of labeled images of gemstones. Paisley leaned over, elbows gently on the counter and studied them. There were so many to choose from. Color might have been the first consideration, then she thought about her birthstone, but a diamond was out of the question.

"Can you give me some idea of price? That might help narrow it down." There were about 36 gems illustrated on the page, but Paisley was sure there were other non-precious stones to choose from. Sure, she could settle for something more affordable, but she could almost hear the necklace whisper to her that it needed a gem. So, gem it would be.

After studying the chart longer than she felt comfortable, she asked Leo if he had a copy of the chart she was looking at. "I could narrow my choices down and send you my top three or four. Will that work? I just can't seem to make a decision right now."

Leo smiled and patted her hand. "I can make it easier for you. This chart is on our website." He handed her another business card from the brass holder. "Our website is listed at the bottom. Take as much time as you need to think about what you want. When you're ready with a few options, contact me for prices. Will that work for you?"

"That will be perfect! It's obvious that I need some time to study them and see which ones appeal to me. Then I'll have to find out if I can afford them."

Leo chuckled, his dark eyes sparkling. "Isn't that always the way?"

"I guess so." Paisley tucked the card into her pocket and reluctantly slid the pad holding the necklace back to Leo. "I'll contact you as soon as I figure it out."

"No hurry, Paisley. Take your time."

"Thanks, Leo. You're a dear."

Halfway to the train station, Paisley came upon a children's shop and stepped inside. It might be just the place to find a few props for the Mother's Day display windows. Colorful and busy, it was full of inviting toys, games, and books. After perusing the book titles, she bought a few toys and a mobile of bees, butterflies, and birds. *These will be perfect for the window display.* The cashier was perky, friendly, and bobbed her head slightly to the jaunty music playing in the store.

On her way out, she typed a few book titles she remembered into the notes app on her phone. They weren't familiar to her but looked like they'd be popular to young book lovers or a just-bathed and ready-for-bed toddler cozied up in the arms of someone ready to read them a story.

Paisley texted her mum on the breezy, cloud-billowing ferry ride across The Solent.

How about pizza tonight? If you want to call an order in to Sammy's, I'll pick it up on my way home. I'm about a half-hour from landing. Sound like a plan?

The bouncing circles told her a reply was on the way; sometimes it stopped, and Paisley could picture her mum thinking about what to say next.

Our usual, right? Anything else besides pizza? Mozzarella sticks? Dipping sauce?

The wind carried Paisley's laugh to the harbour ahead of her. She knew her mum wanted mozzarella sticks but would never request them for herself. Instead, she'd hope Paisley would want some, and they'd share an order.

Sure, Mum! Add an order to the pizza. Sounds yummy!

Okay. I'll place the order in about ten. See you in a bit. XO

As the ferry manoeuvred into place, Paisley admired the newly-emerged greenery on the trees and the vivid, blue sky. Her mind transformed them into green emeralds and blue sapphires until a soft ping alerted her to a message from Finlay. Attached was a video of him, smiling and waving, then focusing on Scott and the electrical panel with wires sticking out of it like the back of a porcupine. She typed quickly, thanking him and asking him to remind Scott they'd need new lines added for a dumb waiter, the extra rooms they were creating, and whatever power they might need outside at some point.

As the ferry bumped against the fenders on the pier, she sent him a selfie and a quick text.

Ferry is docking. Will catch up with you tonight. XOXO

28

Chapter Twenty-Eight

Molly patted the seat on the couch next to her after the pizza dishes had been cleared away. She grabbed her laptop and signed in, rubbing her hands together in anticipation while the device powered up. "Come and sit next to me, Paisley. I want to show you what I've been working on."

She signed in, wrote down the user ID and password, and handed it to Paisley. "In case you want to access this for whatever reason." She steadied the laptop and opened the first file. "I have it set up in sections so that we can add to each generation if we find more information on them. We may find some older ancestors who aren't buried at Thornberry, but I'll show you an example of what I did."

Paisley tensed as she realized that at some point Henry would become part of the conversation, and his death would be revealed to her. For now, she forced herself to focus on the generation Molly was showing her.

"So, here is Cornelius Hix. Born 1710, died 1771. His wife's name was Pearl, and he was the man who built Thornberry Manor. I found some documents on the ancestry site; he built it around 1750. And here is the photo you sent me of his gravestone—nice to have him and his family on the property where he built the home." Molly scrolled to the next page. "Here's a portrait I found and uploaded from the site along with some documents related to the construction." She laughed. "I'm learning some computer lingo, too." Molly turned to Paisley with excitement on her face. "We haven't really scoured the closets and attic at Thornberry. Do you think there's a chance of finding some old portraits of these people there?"

"I hadn't really thought about it, but it's a possibility. Maybe you can come up with me next time, and we can do some rummaging and exploring. If there are, we should protect them and put them on display at some point."

Molly's face looked as though she was calculating

through her calendar. "Well, it will have to be after Mother's Day because it will be quite busy from now until then." She turned her attention back to the screen and scrolled again. "Now, here is Louis Hix. His dates are 1739-1789. He is the son of Cornelius and Pearl, and his wife's name was Philippa. We need a photo of the gravestone if you can find it there."

Then we have Cornelius' other son, William Hix and his wife Prudence. He was born in 1749, and he died in 1825. Boy, these people didn't live into old age, did they?" She hesitated, then continued scrolling. "We have their gravestone."

Paisley nodded, but was focused on all of the wives whose names began with the letter 'P'. Pearl, Philippa, Prudence, and she knew who would probably be next. Polly. Henry's mother. The woman she'd met when she'd traveled back to the year 1829.

"I know, all of these dates can get tedious, but I'm trying to keep things in some sort of order. Anyway, now we come to Flemon Hix, 1804-1856 and his wife Polly. You sent a photo of this gravestone, but part of it is blocked by the tall grass. Can you take another one and send it to me? He married Polly…"

Paisley whispered the name along with her.

"Yes, Polly. How did you know? Oh, the gravestone of course. So, we have Flemon's dates and Polly's are 1809-

1858." Molly held the screen between them and pointed at the photo Paisley had sent. "See here? There's a daughter Phoebe and something else underneath it, but I can't read it. From what I could find on the ancestry site, Phoebe had a daughter named Primrose and they both died the day little Primrose was born. So sad. They probably could have been saved if they'd lived in our time."

Paisley tensed, knowing something about Henry was probably coming next. "I'll send photos of their stone and the other one you need the next time I go back." She got up from the couch, not wanting to hear his date of death. Why was it so painful, something to be avoided at all cost? Of course, he was dead, but some voice inside Paisley told her she mustn't know. Not yet. "Want anything? I'm getting a refill of water."

"No, thanks. I'll keep going. So, then there's Henry, who's probably on the stone but didn't show up in the photo. He was born in 1829, and he died…"

Paisley timed the plugging of her ears perfectly. Humming softly, she missed the date and stayed in the kitchen until her mum moved on to other details about Thornberry. "I love the roses and that orange tree. How old do you suppose they are?"

"Oh, climbing roses can live 50 years or more. The ones you've been pruning could be the descendants of generations going back a hundred years or more. The orange tree? Well, they can live about as long, but they're a single tree, not an offshoot of an older one. So that's probably a more recent addition and not as historically significant as the roses."

"Is there a way to find out what kind of roses they are?"

"Perhaps. But if they're old, they may not be in the current catalogs or nurseries. You could take a leaf sample to the local nursery or wait until they bloom, if we're lucky enough. That might help them identify what variety they are. Maybe they have a list of antique varieties." Molly looked up from her laptop. "I'd wait until they bloom, if they're going to. Fingers crossed."

Paisley set her glass down on the kitchen counter. It had been a long travel day, and she was desperate to crawl into bed and get some sleep. At the same time, she didn't want to discourage her mum on something in which she was so invested; it was her family, after all. And Paisley's. "I'm going to take a quick shower, and then we can finish looking at your ancestry project if you want."

What should have been a relaxing, tension-easing shower turned into a sudsy, soapy argument of wills. Should she tell her mum about the necklace? Yes? No! She said she'd explain about it when she got home. She'd always been able to trust her mum to keep a secret, but this went above and beyond the random, run-of-the-mill, everyday variety. Maybe that was all the more reason to confide in her. Once more she heard the whispered warning. *Keep it secret. Keep it safe.*

"It will be all right," she answered back. Decision made, she toweled off and hurried into her pyjamas. She'd tell her mum and swear her to secrecy. It was probably some one-time wrinkle in the universe, but at least she'd have someone to confide in about it. Paisley rounded the corner of the short hall leading to the living room, inhaling a deep breath as she readied herself to start the conversation.

For now, the decision had been made for her when she found her mum snoozing on the couch with the cosy, green throw tucked around her. Paisley shut down the laptop and gently nudged Molly's shoulder. "C'mon, Mum. Time for bed."

29

Chapter Twenty-Nine

In the week leading up to the trip to Thornberry, Paisley wrestled with her bulging email inbox, answering questions and marking up photos from Scott and Frank as they made steady progress on the electrical and plumbing. She'd submitted the quarterly report with monthly attachments to the Historic England Board and asked them if they needed anything additional from her. Her mum would be coming with this trip, and Paisley wanted to be able to focus on something other than paperwork and emails.

"Do you know anything about dumb waiters?" she asked Finlay as they made the now-familiar trip from the train station to Thornberry. "It doesn't have to be huge, but we need to figure out where it will go and rough-in the space for it."

"We can ask Scott. He's probably installed a few."

"I can't get over how green everything is," Molly piped up from the back seat of the van and made a soft, swooning sound when they turned onto the drive leading to Thornberry. "Oh, it's just so beautiful! Look at the leaves popping out on the trees, the grass greening up, and the lake is plump and full."

Finlay carried in their bags and looked at his watch. "I've got a few things to do this afternoon, but I can bring dinner by this evening. Why don't you call in your order and I'll pick it up and deliver?"

"What would you like?" Paisley asked.

"Surprise me," Finlay said with a wink and a smile. "See you two later."

Paisley settled her mum in the bedroom she'd been using and took the smaller one at the opposite end of the hall for herself. "So, where would you like to start?" she asked when they met in the upstairs hallway.

"Oh, the attic! Have you been up there?"

"Can't say that I have. I've been too busy with the

other floors." Paisley handed her mum a bottle of water. "Let's see what we can find."

The access to the attic was a small, narrow stairway behind a door next to the bedroom where Paisley was staying. "I don't know if there are any lights up here," Paisley said as they climbed the dusty, wooden stairs.

"Well, if there aren't any windows, we'll have to get some flashlights. Or maybe Scott can get us an extension cord long enough to reach downstairs so we can plug in a lamp."

"There are windows. Small, but every bit helps," Paisley said as she reached the top of the stairs and turned the corner. She took Molly's arm and guided her to a safe spot away from the stairs. "I think an extension cord might be a good idea; we may be up here for some time. Look at all this stuff—it looks like it hasn't been touched in years."

Everything was covered in monochromatic shades of grey dust, depending on where the shadows and light fell on them—furniture, trunks, boxes full of who-knows-what, and some odd items like a dressmaker's mannequin and a treadle sewing machine. Molly sneezed. "I think we should get rid of the dust first. Didn't you say you bought a new vacuum cleaner?"

"I did. But we need power up here first. I'll go down to the kitchen and see if Scott might have left an extension cord that we can borrow."

"While you're doing that, I'll find a floor lamp. It'll make working up here a lot easier, especially if it clouds over or if we end up working later in the day."

"Got one!" Paisley called as she climbed the stairs, dragging it behind her like a neon yellow snake. "I'm glad Scott has a 30-meter cord. I'll text him and let him know we're using it. Maybe he can bring an extra until we're done up here or until I can buy one of our own." In her other hand, Paisley had a broom, a bucket of rags, and dusting spray.

Molly set the floor lamp next to the railing. "Let's see if we can get these windows open. It will help with all of the dust we're going to raise."

An hour later, they stood back and surveyed the result of their efforts. Paisley flicked a clump of dust from her mum's shoulder and gave her a hug. "I didn't count on having to do all of this, but I'm not surprised. I guess I thought someone had been up here and maintained it."

Molly untied the rag covering her nose and mouth. "Well, it's done now and looks so much better. Now we can see what we've got up here." She walked among the now-dusted scattering of boxes, crates, and furniture. "We might be able to use some of this furniture in the new bedrooms you're creating. Maybe we should put everything we think we can use on one side and sort through the rest. Some things might be worth keeping—what's left we can either donate or toss."

"This trunk is beautiful," Paisley said as she pulled it into the middle of the room. It had oak framework and bracing, and in between were sections of thin, embossed metal decorated in a swirling pattern of flowers, leaves, and vines. She carefully lifted the lid and leaned it back, ensuring it didn't fall back and snap off. "With a good cleaning, this would be beautiful in one of the guest rooms."

The lightweight, wooden tray held carefully folded clothing that would have belonged to a woman—nightgowns, stockings, and two beautifully-woven shawls. Under the tray was a familiar object that made Paisley gasp. There was no mistaking the muted, floral print dress she'd worn in 1829.

"What is it?" her mum asked.

Paisley found a logical explanation without revealing her secret. "This dress. It's so beautiful and must be really old." She handed it to her mum. "Don't you think?"

"Oh, I think so. Let's take these clothes downstairs and lay them out somewhere. Then how about some lunch? After that, I think we should go outside and get some fresh air and sunshine. How about a walk to the cemetery? We can take another look at who is buried there and get the photos and dates we need."

Paisley swallowed hard as she draped the dress over the couch in the drawing room, the day playing out in her mind as clear and sharp as if it was yesterday with little Phoebe running around and baby Henry in her arms. Then her mind displayed an image of the stone that she was desperately trying to avoid—the monument marking the grave of Henry Hix. When her mum turned away, she shook her head in frustration and confusion. What was the driving force behind her need to *not* know when he died? What did it matter? There were about a dozen graves in the cemetery, all people who were related to her in one way or another on the gnarled, weathered branches of her family tree. What was it about Henry?

30

Chapter Thirty

Molly handed Paisley a biscuit as they passed through the conservatory on their way to the cemetery. Finlay had fashioned a shelf of wooden planks and bricks, set it against the south-facing wall, and filled it with the sun-loving pansies and lavender that had been wintering indoors. She stopped to inspect the orange tree; it was leafing out and thriving in its protective, sunny spot against the stone wall next to the conservatory entrance. "Oh, it looks so happy here. No blossoms though, so most likely no oranges this year. Maybe next, if we take good care of it."

Paisley glanced up at the side of the house where the roses she'd pruned clung to the grey, rough stone. "Look at all of the new growth, Mum. Do you think they'll bloom?"

Molly smiled as she looked at the roses climbing the house and the stone walls enclosing what might have once been a sitting area outside the conservatory. "I think we might be in luck there, Paisley. Let's pick up some food for them and the orange tree. Maybe we can hitch a ride with Finlay to Keighley one day and do some shopping."

"Good idea. We can start a list after we ask him. He'll be back tonight with dinner."

"You two seem to be getting on quite well." Paisley heard the smile in her mum's voice and couldn't hide her own.

"We are, Mum. Finlay's a great guy."

"Is it serious? Your relationship?" As they approached the gate to the cemetery, Molly pulled a small notebook from her pocket and shifted gears. "I suppose I'll interrogate you about that later; for now, I want to get these family members documented for my ancestry project." Molly opened the gate, and the soft, warm breeze ushered them inside. "Maybe we should start at one end and work our way through so we don't miss anyone."

The grass would be ready to mow soon, and the weeds and ivy that clung to some of the stones would need to be trimmed away. They could all use a good cleaning, but not today. Paisley and her mum worked systematically from south to north, photographing and speculating on the lives of their ancestors. "Here's Cornelius and his wife, Pearl. Cornelius is 1710-1771, and Pearl is 1720-1752. He built Thornberry Manor, so we have him to thank, I guess." Molly leaned forward and looked at the dates. "Pearl died when she was just 32. How sad. I wonder what happened."

"Well, a lot of people didn't live as long as they do now, but you might find something in your research—maybe a death certificate that might list the cause of death?"

Molly jotted in her notebook. "Yes, I need to research that bit." She sat down next to Paisley on the grass in front of the stone. "If I remember correctly, Cornelius built Thornberry around 1750. That would make it how old?"

Paisley did the calculation on her phone. "Two hundred seventy-four years. Wow, it's held up well." She looked back at the house. "Don't you wonder who might have visited, been in those rooms, and walked around the grounds? I mean, there were some pretty important people living then who might have come to visit." She did a quick, Internet search and read some of the results to her mum. "These are all in the 1800s, but listen to what was going on in the book world—*Pride and Prejudice* was published in 1813, and Mary Shelley wrote *Frankenstein* in 1818." Paisley shivered a bit while reading the last part, picturing the copy hidden in plain sight on the bookshelf in the study. "Did we document William and Prudence Hix? They'd be next in line after Cornelius and Pearl."

"No, but let's see if we can find them." Molly jumped up and started searching at the point where they'd left off. "Here they are. William and Prudence—Cornelius and Pearl's son and his wife. William is 1749-1825, and Prudence is 1750-1825. They died the same year; I wonder how far apart. I'll have to do some research when I get home. Right now, it hits me as something romantically sad."

Paisley photographed the stone and the others as they made their way from one end to the other. "I'm not sure about this one. Based on the dates, it could be a relative of William's—in his generation, but not a direct family member. Louis Hix is 1739-1789 and his wife Philippa is 1752-1804. They must be related, but I'm not sure how. They were both gone before the books we talked about were published, but they could have known the women as young girls and their families. Fascinating, isn't it?"

Paisley scrolled through the photos on her phone. "I know it might be just a coincidence, but all of the wives we've found so far have names that start with 'P'." It was both puzzling and fascinating. Was there any significance to it? *So, the necklace could have belonged to any one of them, all of them (in succession), or none of them.* Perhaps they'd find an old portrait with one of the women wearing it. She made a mental note to check the portraits already hanging throughout the house along with any they might find in the attic. It was becoming her own personal mystery and mission.

The afternoon sun slipped low enough to transform into a mosaic filter through the trees beyond the west end of the cemetery. "Let's get these last few done, Mum, then we can go inside. I think we've fulfilled our fresh air/sunshine requirement for the day, and we've only got a few more stones to photograph."

"Oh, before I forget, let me place the order for our dinner. Then I can let Finlay know, and he can give them a timeline for picking it up."

After placing the order, Paisley moved to the new stone that stood out from the others. Paisley took a photo and stepped back as Molly leaned in to read the name. "Oh, this is John B. Hicks, the last resident of Thornberry. Wife Margaret and their daughter Rachel who died in 1991. I wonder if it's her room that has the feminine décor. Perhaps it was John and Margaret who lived here before us since Rachel died before both of them." She studied the name etched in the mottled stone. "Did you notice that the spelling of his last name has changed. His predecessors were Hix and he's listed as Hicks. I wonder why that is."

"I'm not sure, but I can check census records and other documents to see if the spelling changed with him."

"He's the one whose passing made it possible for Thornberry to come to us," Paisley said. "So, I thank him for that." She turned in a slow circle, looking at all of the stones. "And all of those who came before us."

Molly walked toward the gate, then stopped and turned. "We need another photo of Flemon and Polly's stone because the one you took before didn't show all of the names and dates."

Paisley felt her chest tighten and sweat form on her palms. There was no getting past it, but maybe her mum could take the photo, and it wouldn't be anywhere where she could see it. It was worth a try. "Mum, you take it, okay?"

"Why? You've taken all of the others."

Paisley glanced at the side of the stone. "It's hard to explain, Mum, and this is not the time or place. There's something about that family that I can't face and don't want to know about. Maybe if there's time before Finlay shows up, I'll do my best to tell you why. But for now, can you just take the photo on your phone and not tell me anything that's on it? Please?"

Molly's breath puffed with confusion and frustration. "I don't understand, Paisley, but I'll do as you ask. For now. But I think at some point I deserve an explanation."

"I will, Mum. I promise." Paisley stood by the gate while Molly took the last photo. She forced a cheerful lilt to her voice and put her arm through Molly's as they left the cemetery. "Well, we have that all taken care of, and you have more data for your research project."

As they neared the house, dust curls announced Finlay's arrival. Paisley let out a huge, quiet sigh of relief. *Perfect timing. Maybe Mum will forget about Flemon and Polly's stone, at least for a little while.*

"Dinner delivery!" Finlay called as he climbed out of the truck. "I hope you're hungry."

31

Chapter Thirty-One

The afternoon at the cemetery had been warm and pleasant enough, but it felt good to be sitting in front of a fire, cuddled next to Finlay with a full stomach and a glass of wine. Molly had excused herself after dinner and turned in early; traveling from Bonchurch, exploring the attic, and documenting the stones in the cemetery had worn her out.

"Don't you wonder sometimes how many people have been here before us—enjoying a fire from this very spot? And who they were?" Paisley pointed at both sides of the fireplace at the framed faces watching her. "I have no idea who those people are. Do you think there might be some names or dates on them?"

Finlay laughed softly and hugged her closer to him. "Do we have to inspect them now? Haven't you had enough for one day?" After a soft, lingering kiss, he refilled her wine. "Besides, they're not going anywhere; they'll be there tomorrow if you're still intent on finding out."

"At some point, yes," Paisley whispered, leaning in for another kiss. "But not tonight. They've been here for years; you're right, another night or two won't matter."

"Come here, then," Finlay growled softly, his passion becoming more intense and insistent.

"What?" Paisley sat up and looked over the back of the couch at the open door toward the staircase. "Here? Now? What if my mum comes down?"

Finlay groaned, then stood and pulled her up with him. "Well, you could go up and see if she's sleeping. While you're gone, I can scope out a more suitable place—more discreet, anyway."

"Deal!" Paisley raced up the stairs and tiptoed toward the east-facing bedroom where her mum was staying. Poised outside the door, she smiled as she listened to the soft, rhythmic snoring that was so familiar to her.

She returned and gave an enthusiastic thumbs-up to an empty drawing room. "Where are you?" she asked in a hushed whisper. "Finlay?" Her answer came in the form of a kiss on the back of her neck. She spun around. "Where did you go?"

"You'll find out." He took her by the hand. "Come with me."

Finlay led her across the drawing room and out the door onto the wrap-around balcony, following it next to the house and around the corner.

"It's a bit brisk for outdoor sex, don't you think?" Paisley whispered as she shivered with a mix of chill and excitement. She'd never had sex outside with anyone. "Assuming that's your plan, I mean." The full moon overhead negated the need for any help finding their way, and Finlay tightened his grip on her hand as he rounded the corner.

"It is, indeed."

It was calm and sheltered on the back side of the house, and a surprising, welcome heat radiated from the stone wall where Finlay stopped and pressed her hand against it. "It's the back side of the fireplace; feel how warm it is." He reached for the blanket he'd rolled up next to the wall and wrapped it around her, sending both of them into a frenzy of hushed moaning and passionate kissing as they tugged on each other's clothes.

"Something tells me this is going to be a quick and

done," Paisley blurted, muffling her laugh with a hand over her mouth as she let the blanket fall and pulled Finlay down with her.

"Probably a blessing in disguise," Finlay whispered as he wrapped his arms around her and settled himself between her legs. "That way, we won't have to get completely naked and compromise our extremities—those that aren't being used, that is."

"I'll bear that in mind," Paisley murmured with feigned formality followed by a giggle.

The amber, non-judgmental moon surreptitiously peeked in the spaces between the random, luminous clouds at the couple making love on the balcony below. Paisley glanced at it once and felt as if it was smiling down on them—and smiled back.

Finlay held her close against the night air and anything else that could possibly come between them; despite the chill, Paisley basked in the safe, secure feeling and the warmth of his embrace. In a small, moonlit space between climax and cleave, she heard him whisper through her tousled hair, "I love you."

32

Chapter Thirty-Two

While Scott worked inside on the space for the new dumb waiter, Paisley and her mum walked down to the lake. It was the perfect time to wander and explore before the predicted afternoon rain arrived from the west. A large raft of mallards broke off into pairs as they approached, quacking in subdued alarm, but unwilling to take flight and leave the safety and peace of their nesting area. The trees circling the lake were alive with woodpeckers, robins, and other birds searching for seeds and insects in the branches and in the litter-strewn undergrowth.

"Just listen to them—isn't it lovely?" Molly whispered.

"It is, Mum." She put her arm around her shoulder and hugged her. "And it's all yours. Can you believe it?"

"Sometimes. Almost." With a smile, she took Paisley's arm in hers. "C'mon. Let's go 'round the back and see what we can find."

What looked like an overgrown lawn gradually revealed its secrets as bumpy ridges of lawn turned out to be age-old furrows. Molly pulled at a section of weeds and overgrown grass with delight. "Why, it's a kitchen garden! Or, it used to be." She looked around for anything vaguely familiar, then pulled up a stalk with an excited grin on her face. "Rhubarb! Probably gone wild, but I think we can restore order and see what else might be hiding under the weeds. Perhaps one of the tenants would be willing to come and mow it. Once that's done, we can see if there's anything salvageable before tilling." Molly straightened up and pointed to the back of the plot. "Those look like apple trees. Some pruning and fertilizer might bring them 'round." As she walked back to where Paisley was standing, she poked and pulled at places that caught her eye. "Do you suppose Finlay knows one of the tenants who might be willing to help us? We could offer some extra pay for his time and trouble, of course."

"Sure, Mum. Let's ask him tonight."

Molly followed Paisley's gaze to the back of the house. "What are you looking at? Is there something wrong?"

Paisley tempered her smile, sending most of it to the inner sanctum of her heart. The balcony where she and Finlay had made love under the moonlight stood silent and stoic, the ancient, grey stone was a silent witness, willing and able to keep their secret. "No, nothing's wrong. I'm just glad the house is in such good condition. Sure, we have some major work to do on the inside, but I'm happy that the exterior is still so beautiful."

As they continued to explore, the shifting wind ushered in a bank of lead-colored clouds. "Looks like the rain will be here soon," Molly said, tucking wisps of hair behind her ears. "Time to head in, I think. Let's have lunch in the drawing room, and you can tell me about the necklace. You've started the story so many times, but something always interrupts us. I really want to hear about it."

Paisley felt her body tense as her mind fought the warning she'd been given time and time again. She'd kept the secret long enough, and she knew she could trust her mum to do the same. Part of her was desperate to tell someone what had happened, even though she was pretty sure it would never happen again—the broken emerald was evidence enough.

"Sure, Mum. We have all afternoon."

They met up with Scott in the kitchen, packing up his tools and preparing to leave. "Oh, I was just coming to find you. The rough-in is done for the dumb waiter; it should be here sometime next week." He shut his tool box with a snap and grunted a bit as he set it on the end of the wooden table. "While I wait for the dumb waiter, I'll continue working on the bedrooms and bathrooms and get them wired and ready for plumbing. I hope you don't mind if I head out for the rest of the day. I just got a call from a lady who lost the power at her house, and I want to get there before the rain does."

"No, that's fine, Scott. Help her out and we'll see you tomorrow?" Paisley could tell her mum was listening as she pulled lunch fixings out of the refrigerator.

"Yes, tomorrow. I have some materials to pick up first thing, then I'll be over."

"Sounds great. Thanks so much, Scott. We'll see you then."

"Goodbye, Paisley. Mrs. Venne."

Molly gave him a grateful smile. "Goodbye, Scott. Take care out there."

Paisley built a small fire in the drawing room while her mum finished preparing tuna melts. "I know we probably don't need a fire, but it may cool off, and it's better than sitting in front of an empty fireplace."

"I agree. It adds a bit of cosy atmosphere."

Paisley took the last bite of her lunch, leaned back in her chair, and studied the faces in the portraits on the wall looking back at her. "We need to really look at these paintings, Mum. They might have names or dates on them that will tie them to the research you're doing."

Molly nodded as she bit into a crisp, snappy apple. "You're right, but I want to hear about the necklace first."

Paisley took a deep breath, then exhaled. Her mum was right. She'd held on to her secret long enough; if she was going to tell anyone the astonishing story of what happened to her, it would be her mum. "Okay, but you have to promise me something first."

"What's that?"

"You have to promise not to breathe a word of this to anyone. Not a single person. Promise?"

"Yes, of course, but I didn't know what you're about to tell me would be that earth-shattering."

"Just promise, Mum."

"All right, all right. I promise."

"Okay. Well, I'll start at the beginning."

"That's probably a good place," Molly said, interrupting her.

"Mum, you have to just listen and not jump in, okay?"

Molly raised her hands in a gesture of surrender, put a small piece of wood on the fire, and settled back into her chair.

Paisley decided to make what she was about to say as straightforward and matter-of-fact as possible; how else could she deal with something so impossible to explain away? "So, the first time I came here and was looking around, I found the necklace in the wooden wardrobe in the room where you're staying. It was hanging on a nail, and I would never have found it if my hair hadn't gotten snagged."

Molly remained silent except for intermittent gasps, incredulous expressions, and at one point holding her hand over her mouth to keep from speaking. "Are you sure?" she whispered when Paisley finally stopped speaking. "Are you sure it wasn't a daydream or some sort of imagining?"

"I'm sure, Mum. It was as real as you and I sitting together right now."

Molly politely shook her head. "You know, people think things that happen to them are real when they're half-asleep or desperately want whatever they're thinking about to come true..."

Paisley stood and pulled her mum up. "Come here. Come with me." Still holding her hand, she led the way into the study and posted her mum in front of the bookshelves. Quickly scanning the left side, she found the book and handed it to her. "Look at the title page."

Molly uttered the name with whispered reverence when she found the page. "Mary Shelley." She turned to Paisley. "You met her. You actually met her? In 1829?"

"I did."

Molly hugged the book, then handed it to Paisley. "You need to tell me more about her, but for now you need to keep this somewhere safe, where no one else can find it."

"Yeah, I'm trying to figure that out. How do you look after and hide something like this? A safe deposit box at the bank? I know I have to protect it, but I hate to think of something this precious sitting in the dark, in a cold, steel box somewhere."

Paisley returned it to the shelf. "I'll leave it here for now. You and I are the only ones who know about it."

"And what about the necklace? Will it still ... work?"

"I have no clue, but I doubt it. The emerald is just a bunch of crumbs now, if it had anything to do with what happened. Leo from Theodore & Son is working to find a replacement for it, and it will probably become just a piece of old jewellery again."

"So, how does that tie in with your reluctance to see Henry's death date on the stone in the cemetery?"

"I'm not sure, but something tells me not to know. I'm going to ask Finlay to cover it, so I don't see it by accident. I don't know how I'm going to explain it to him without telling him the story, but it needs to be covered."

"I can cover it with something. We can find something in the conservatory, even a scrap of wood. You won't have to ask Finlay. We can do it this afternoon. Right now."

"Really?"

"Of course, Paisley." Molly got up and gathered up the lunch dishes. "You take the tray downstairs, and I'll see what I can find to cover the date on Henry's side of the stone."

"Do you remember which one it is?"

"I think so. You can come with me close enough to show me the stone but far enough away so you don't see the date. Come on. Let's do it now before the rain sets in."

33

Chapter Thirty-Three

It was a crudely-constructed notice, but it served its purpose. Tied in place with a length of rope, a piece of plywood covered the left-hand side of the stone with the instruction *Do Not Remove* written on a piece of cardboard. "There, that should do it." Molly stood back in the heavy drizzle and admired what she'd been able to do with the limited resources available.

Paisley stepped up and tested the tautness of the rope. "That ought to hold. Thanks, Mum."

"You're welcome, Poppet. Now, let's get out of the

wet." Light rain tapped on the leaves of the trees, urging them through the gate and into the conservatory.

Paisley stopped in the doorway and looked back at the orange tree soaking up the soft, gentle rain. "Look, Mum, it's almost completely leafed out and looks so happy there. Do you think we'll get any oranges?"

"Perhaps, but I wouldn't expect too much of it after being neglected for so long. Producing fruit takes a lot of energy. If it was going to produce fruit, I think we'd have blossoms or at least buds." Molly reached out and touched the soil at the base of the tree. "Let's just keep feeding and tending it, and we'll see."

As Paisley pulled the door closed behind them, her phone alerted her with a message. She smiled when she saw that it was Finlay.

Molly gently tugged on Paisley's sleeve. "If that's Finlay, ask him if he's coming tonight. If he is, would he mind bringing dinner if we order online? We should have dinner there at some point, but I'm tired and too lazy right now. If he's willing, have him order something for himself, of course—it's the least we can do for him picking up and bringing it to us."

Paisley started a fire in the study, and the pair pulled their chairs next to each other and cozied up in front of the fireplace. "Change of scenery, Mum," Paisley explained with a smile as they settled into the deep, soft cushions. "Giving the drawing room a bit of a break. Besides, we haven't spent much time in here."

"Not since you showed me *that*," Molly said, pointing to the book on the shelf. "Part of me is afraid to come in here, afraid it might be gone, afraid it isn't real."

"Well, it's there, and it *is* real. And you have to make sure to keep it tucked away in some secret compartment in your brain, so you don't give it away." Paisley tensed and turned to face her mum. "It's really important; you know that, right?"

"I know, Pet, but it's just you and me right now, so we can talk about it, okay?"

Paisley nodded as she studied the small volume hiding in plain sight—left set of shelves, second shelf from the bottom, fourth book from the left. "Sometimes I wish it had never happened to me. It's amazing and all, but I don't know what to do with it."

Molly took her hand. "You don't need to do anything just now. We have enough other things to deal with that can keep us busy."

"I need to figure out a safer place for it. I did ask Finlay if he could make locking doors with glass panels to protect and display them at the same time. There are other, old books here that are just as valuable in their own way.

Maybe having all of them under lock and key will be enough."

"Does he know about your book? About any of it?"

Paisley forced herself to be patient. *Maybe I shouldn't have told her. It would be better if she didn't know anything. That way, I wouldn't have to risk her unintentionally saying something. Now she has to bear part of the burden.* She took a deep breath and forced the lurking tension and frustration from her voice. "You're the only one who knows, Mum. You and me. And we have to keep it that way, okay?"

"I know," she whispered. "I know what you're up against. But it's pretty exciting, too—you have to admit that." She got up and moved to the book shelf. "Can I look at it once more?"

"Of course, Mum."

Molly opened the book to the title page where it had been signed for Paisley. "Tell me about her. What was Mary Shelley like?"

"I met her in this very room, close to where you are standing. When I came into the room, she was talking to Flemon Hix. He introduced us, we talked for a bit, and then she signed the copy she was holding and gave it to me." Paisley told her mum every detail she remembered about Mary, the other visitors, and the furnishings and general appearance of Thornberry Manor. "Remember the dress we found in the attic that day? That's what I was wearing."

Molly gasped. "Really? I need to see it again. Do you think it has anything to do with traveling to the past? If you put the dress on, would it happen again?"

"I don't know, but I don't think so. I think the necklace is key, or at least a major player. I don't know who it belonged to, where it came from, or how it had the ability to transport me. All we know is it was probably made for someone whose name started with the letter 'P'."

"And we're finding out that there were a lot of women in our family tree whose name started with that letter."

As Paisley added another chunk of oak to the fire, they were interrupted by the sound of an approaching vehicle on the gravel drive. She went to the window, her heart-warming at the sight of Finlay walking toward the door with takeaway bags in his hands. "Finlay's here with dinner."

Molly gave the book a gentle hug and quickly returned it to its place on the shelf. "Thank you, Poppet, for telling me your story. It's safely tucked away now, on the shelf and in a special place in my memory."

Dinner was a relaxed, laughter-filled evening in front of the fire in the study with a clutter of takeaway boxes, beverage containers, and blackberry crumble set aside to enjoy later.

"We've got a group from Florida who thought that May in central England is the same temperature and climate as May in Florida. I had to make an unscheduled stop at a shopping centre to let them shop for warmer clothes." He leaned forward to put another piece of wood on the fire. "So, what's been happening here?"

"Well, we're trying to get some things sorted before I have to go back on Saturday. Alice has been doing a great job at the shop, but I need to get back and take care of business."

Paisley gathered up the empty food containers and returned them to the delivery bag. "Wow. The day after tomorrow. Time flies up here; we seem to just get started on things, and then it's time to leave."

"You don't have to leave, Paisley. I can get home on my own."

"No way, Mum. I'm not letting you travel all that way alone. I'll go back with you and help in the shop until you get caught up. Then I'll come back and see where we are with things."

"I can keep up with Scott and Frank on the electrical and plumbing," Finlay said. "Let me know what you want them to finish up and start on next, and I'll continue on with them. What do you want me to work on while you're gone?"

They formulated a plan over their dessert of

blackberry crumble and trips to the kitchen and upstairs rooms that were in the process of renovation. "I need to send reports to the Historic England Grant Office and make sure they have everything they need to keep us going. I'll do that when I get home; it's been going well so far, so I guess they're happy with what's happening at Thornberry."

Molly got up with a yawn. "Well, I've had enough for today. Thank you, Finlay, for bringing dinner and for everything else you've been doing. If I don't see you tomorrow, I'll see you Saturday morning around 8:30?"

"Sure thing, Mrs. Venne."

"Molly. Please call me Molly."

"Sure thing, Molly. Thank you for feeding me and for including me in your vision for Thornberry Manor." His blue eyes warmed when he looked at Paisley. "I told Hazel, my mum, about you and Paisley. She'd like to meet both of you sometime."

"That would be wonderful—I'd love to meet her. We both would. One of the times I'm up here we'll have to get together—maybe dinner at the inn?"

"I'm sure we can arrange something."

"Well, I'll say goodnight then."

"Goodnight, Mum."

Finlay raised his hand in a gentle wave. "Goodnight, Molly."

Finlay and Paisley settled together in the larger of the two chairs facing the fireplace. "It's getting harder and harder, bringing you to the train station, not knowing when I'll see you again." He punctuated it with a long, tender kiss as his arms enfolded her in a tight, emotional embrace. "I hope it won't always be this way."

"Me, either. I'm hoping that if I can get Thornberry up and running, I can spend the majority of my time here and help Mum in Bonchurch when she needs it."

"Have you talked to her about it?"

"Not yet. I'm hoping once I get the house in order, it will come as a natural progression, and she'll see the logic in it. Maybe she'll decide…"

Paisley's phone interrupted her train of thought. "What the heck?" She looked at the name on the screen of her phone. "Why is Leo calling me now?"

"Who is Leo?"

"He's the jeweller in London repairing a necklace I brought to him. Let me see what he wants; it should just take a minute." Her finger trembled a bit as she tapped the screen. "Hello, Leo."

"Hello. Is this Paisley Venne? It's Leo, from Theodore & Son in London."

"Hi, Leo. Your name popped up on my phone. What's up?"

226

"Well, I'm afraid I have some bad news." Paisley's mind jumped to the necklace as fear cinched a knot in her stomach, but she forced herself to wait for Leo to speak again.

"There was a break-in at the shop a short while ago."

"What? What happened?"

"The door was forced open, and our cameras show two figures smashing and grabbing what they could. The police just left, and we're trying to put the shop back together and secure it as best we can for tonight."

"Oh, Leo. I'm so sorry."

"We're doing our best, Ms. Venne, but it's with regret that I have to inform you that so far we have not recovered your necklace."

34

Chapter Thirty-Four

Page-Turner Books was closed on Sunday, so it was the perfect time to get the display windows changed and merchandise tables ready. One window would pay tribute to King Charles III, since his official birthday was the 15th of June. A bunting was hung in the window, framed photos of Charles at different ages were placed among small flags on stands, and books featuring the monarch were strategically placed on easels or stacked between bookends.

Paisley decided to dedicate one of the display tables in the center of the store to books featuring the royal family in case shoppers wanted to read something about other past and present royals. She had Union Jack flags ready to hang above the table to call attention to the contents of the display.

The other window was set up as a tribute to fathers, since the 16th was Father's Day. Paisley's heart lurched as she set a framed photo of her father reading to her in the display window. Neither of them were authors, but it was her way of remembering and paying tribute to him. He would have been okay with it, and it brought back memories of story time before bed. After some research on the computer, she discovered authors who had famous fathers and printed out short narratives to display alongside the books; it would provide an interesting take on a typical Father's Day offering of books.

She started with *A Tale of Two Cities*, *Oliver Twist* and *David Copperfield* by Charles Dickens and added *Dickens' Dictionary of London* written by his son, Charles Dickens, Jr.

Joseph Hillman King used the pen name Joe Hill to set himself apart from his father, Stephen King. She thought readers might find that bit of trivia fascinating as she gathered up copies of Stephen's *Misery, Blaze,* and *Fairy Tale* to set alongside his son's *The Fireman* and *Full Throttle.*

One, last pairing was that of Arthur Waugh and his two sons, Evelyn and Alec. Arthur's *Poems and Plays* was displayed next to the perhaps better-known works of his sons, *Brideshead Revisited* by Evelyn and *Island in the Sun* by Alec.

Extras and other copies by the authors were stacked on a table beyond the royal display with posters of the writers suspended overhead. After a quick inventory, she logged onto the publishing software and placed an order of additional copies of some of the titles to ensure they had plenty of stock on hand.

She was putting the finishing touches on the display tables when her mum came down with a tray of tea and brownies. "Thanks, Mum." She took a sip, grateful for the cream and bit of sugar her mum knew she liked. "Check out the displays; I think they look pretty good, if I say so myself."

Molly looked at the windows from outside and had tears in her eyes when she returned. "They look beautiful, and that picture of you and your father…"

"I know. At first, I wasn't sure if I should put it there. We're not authors, but he was *my* father, and he did read to me almost every night before bed. I wanted to pay tribute to him and somehow let him know that though he may be gone, he's not forgotten."

"What a sweet sentiment. Even if no one notices, we'll know it's there, and that's all that matters." Molly finished her tea and changed the subject. "Any word from

Leo on your necklace?"

"No, but a part of me wants to pay a visit to Theodore & Son just the same."

Molly shook her head. "Why? It was never appraised or insured, so what would be the point?" She gathered up the dishes and turned toward the stairs. "Perhaps it's for the best. Let it be, wherever it is. I'm sure what happened to you will not happen to anyone else because we think that somehow, it's tied to Thornberry. What are the odds that whoever has the necklace will travel to Thornberry and put it on once they're inside?" Molly turned and sat on the steps with the tray in her lap. "Even then, it might not work, because whoever has it is not a relative. Isn't that what it takes? How it works?"

"I was trying to figure out that part, but I think you're right. Family member, necklace, Thornberry. And something with the letter 'P', which means it probably wouldn't work for you."

"You're probably right. At any rate, I'd be afraid to try."

Paisley looked around the shop. "Looks pretty good, don't you think? I need to get the flags hung over the royals display table, do a quick sweep of the floors, and that should do it. I'll take a couple of photos, post them on our site, and advertise the book events."

Molly smiled as she stood. "I don't know what I'd do without you, Poppet. I can only do so much. I don't have the creative imagination that you have, not to mention your computer skills."

"Well, I'm here and happy to help."

Settled on the couch with the remote in her hand, Molly hesitated and turned to Paisley with a look of concern shadowing her features. "What about Thornberry? What will happen when it's ready to open? Will you move up there permanently? How will I manage without you?"

Paisley saved the last update to the website and closed down her laptop. "It'll sort itself out, Mum. We're just getting started, and there are still a lot of steps between now and when we finally open. I would never leave you on your own if you needed my help—remember that, okay?"

Molly pressed her hands to her tear-filled eyes. "I know. I just worry sometimes."

Paisley leaned over and hugged her mum. "You worry too much. About everything. So, take that off of your list, okay?"

Molly nodded, wiped her eyes, and handed Paisley the remote. "You choose. I'm just happy to be here with you. Doesn't matter what we watch."

Paisley felt her phone vibrate with an incoming message. It was Finlay, but she chose to ignore it for now and muted her phone. She needed to be fully present with her mum and to reassure her that with all that was going on, she was still important enough to have Paisley all to herself once in a while. "Now then, let's see what choices we have. Stop me if there's something you'd like to watch."

They spent the rest of the afternoon and early evening in front of the TV. Dinner was leftover pasta, bread sticks, and brownies for dessert—not a green vegetable in sight. Molly fell asleep halfway through the second movie and woke up when Paisley shut off the TV. "We should probably go to bed, Mum. Tomorrow's Monday and the first day of our promotion. Let's hope it's a success."

Molly yawned and moved out from under the afghan, carefully folding it and laying it over the back of the couch. "You're right. Monday morning will come soon enough."

"You go ahead and use the bathroom first; I'll clean up these dishes and turn the lights off."

"Thanks, Poppet. I won't be long—I'm too tired to dawdle."

"Goodnight, Mum. I love you," Paisley called after her, smiling as she watched her shuffling along as she steered her slippers down the hall.

"I love you, too, Paisley. See you in the morning."

While she waited, Paisley stood at the windows

overlooking the street below and expanse of water beyond. It was quiet, too, as if it had been tucked in for the night. There was barely a ripple, just a gentle, undulating motion as if the sea itself were breathing softly as it settled to sleep with the nearly-full moon and stars watching over it.

After a quick shower, Paisley climbed into bed and pulled out her phone to read the text from Finlay.

Hi, Sweet! Missed you the moment you stepped on the train. I'm working with Scott and Frank to keep things moving along, and they're helping me get the conservatory panels installed. It's going to be beautiful—can't wait for you to see it. Trying to beat the rain that's predicted for the weekend.

Things are busy at the inn, so there isn't much down time. That's a good thing, but what I wouldn't give for a day with nothing to do. Hope all is well in Bonchurch. Feels like a world away.

Much love,

Finlay

Paisley smiled at the photo he'd sent of himself under the skeletal framework of the conservatory. Wooden crates behind him likely held the etched, glass panels that would be lifted into place. *I hope there are a few extra, just in case.*

Hi, Handsome! Feel like I'm living in two, separate worlds. Here at home, and Thornberry. Was I crazy to think I could take it on? Times like this, I think so and wonder where I'll end up. Set up a book promotion display for the shop — will send pics tomorrow. Probably a quick trip to London, but not sure when that will be. Can you tell I'm tired and doubting everything I do? Could use a hug right now. One of those all night, wrapped in your arms kind.

Love,

Paisley XO

She drifted off to sleep listening to the soft, onshore breeze whispering at her window and decided that after the bookshop events of June 15-16, it might be a good time to visit Leo and pay him for the work he'd done on the necklace before it was lost.

35

Chapter Thirty-Five

Paisley smiled to herself as she boarded the ferry Friday morning for the trip to London. Men *did* read, after all, and the crowds in the store for the King's birthday and Father's Day promotion bolstered her confidence regarding the themes and the choices she'd made.

Perhaps holiday/beach reads would be next. She made a mental note to stop by Greville Street Books and see what they were featuring. Summer reads for children might be good with the school year coming to an end in mid-July. One display window for adult readers and one for kids; mid-

June was the perfect time to get started.

Her hunch was right. Greville Street Books' display window had a lawn chair, a multi-colored, opened beach brolly, and pails and shovels on burlap and chiffon sand. Their one, large window combined books for adults and children; Paisley could separate them with the two their shop had. The fabric sand was a good idea; she sent a photo with a text to her mum and asked if they had any at home that could be a stand-in for sand. If not, could she see if Alice had anything, or buy some?

She made a quick tour of the shop, looking at the in-store displays for ideas of something that might work for them. Some of their ideas sparked her own, like easy, no-fuss recipes for summer and grilling cookbooks. Perhaps some hobby-related books would do well; Paisley typed her ideas into the notes app on her phone after stepping outside.

It was a short walk from Greville Street Books to the jewellery store, and Paisley's chest tightened with each step. At one point, she stopped and sat on a bench, forcing herself to take a few, deep breaths and focus on the clouds, the breeze, and the traffic in the street. *Why the panic and anxiety? You're just going to talk to Leo and offer to pay for the work they did on the necklace. Should just be a matter of minutes, and you can be on your way home.* "Fine," she whispered to herself. "Let's get on with it then."

As she approached the store entrance, the fresh paint on the door and new lock were the only signs of repair that Paisley noticed. Everything else related to the robbery had been cleaned up long ago, and Theodore & Son was open for business as usual. She smiled at the soft tinkling of the bell above the door, grateful that the robbers hadn't taken or destroyed it.

A young woman behind the counter greeted her; Paisley noted the name Lucy on her name badge. "Good morning. Can I help you?"

Paisley was thrown off-kilter as she looked around the shop. "Good morning. I'd like to speak to Leo. I'm sorry, I don't know his last name. Is he working today?"

Lucy looked around, then held up a finger for Paisley to wait. "I think he's just finishing his break. Can I let him know who's asking for him?"

"Paisley Venne. Thanks. I can wait. I'm in no hurry, and I don't want to interrupt his break." As the last word left her mouth, Leo emerged from the back room. "Good morning! I hope I didn't impose on your break." Then she lowered her voice to a whisper. She knew she'd addressed it already, but felt the need to clarify. "It feels weird, me calling you Leo. Shouldn't I address you as Mr. something? Mr. Leo?"

"Nonsense." He smiled as he patted his badge. "Leo

is fine."

Paisley thought about it for a moment. Perhaps the first name only on the badges was sort of a security or identity protection mechanism. At any rate, he seemed okay with her referring to him by his first name.

Leo took her hand and held it for a moment, then motioned her over to a section of the counter near the door. "It will be quieter for us to visit here, away from the other customers." He leaned toward her, elbows gently on the counter. His grey hair was combed neatly in place, his eyes full of concern and regret. "I cannot tell you how sorry I am about the loss of your necklace."

"Well, it wasn't your fault, so there's nothing to be sorry for. I'm happy to see that you're open for business, and I hope that those who committed the crime have been found and will face justice."

"The investigation is on-going, and we have some good leads. That's about all I can say at this point."

"I totally understand. I only came by to pay for the work you did on the necklace before it was stolen. I owe you that much."

Leo raised his hands to object, but Paisley had already pulled her debit card from her wallet and was reaching across the counter to hand it to him. "Please. I insist."

In the gesturing and tangle of hands, the card fell from Paisley's grasp and descended into the small sliver of space between the two counters. Leo peered down into the crack, then fell to his knees behind the counter. "Oh, my! I'm so sorry! Let me help you retrieve it."

"I think you're going to need something long and slender to get between the counters," Paisley mused as she squinted into the darkened space.

"I might have just the thing in the back room. I'll be right back." He returned after a few moments with a narrow, metal rod and small flashlight. "This might do the trick."

Paisley crouched down in front of the open space as Leo worked from above, aiming the light into the space and working the debit card out from where it had fallen. After several unsuccessful tries, he handed the flashlight to Paisley. "You shine the light, and I'll work from here to flick it your way." After few more tries, Paisley was able to retrieve a gold ring; on the next try, the card flew onto the floor next to Paisley.

"Got it!" Paisley was about to turn off the flashlight, but something caught her eye, and she continued to peer into the opening. She gasped, put her hand over her mouth, and shone the light into Leo's face. "Keep flicking, Leo. There's something else down there." She aimed the light back into the narrow space between the counters. "Carefully now. Gently, toward me."

She reached in with her index finger, trying to reach the objects. "Once more, Leo, then I think I can grab them." Leo made one last try, and Paisley was able to reach several rings from the darkened space where they had fallen. And one more thing. As she held it up, she flopped into a sitting position on the floor and held the object to her chest.

"Are you all right, Paisley?" Leo hurried from his spot behind the counter and crouched next to her. "What is it?"

Paisley fought the tears, but it was useless. "Oh Leo, if you hadn't been here, you'd never have believed it." She held it out to him and whispered in a trembling voice. "It's my necklace."

The few, remaining customers quickly finished their business and left discreetly while Lucy and the other employees kept a respectful distance. Leo helped her to her feet and gave the necklace a quick examination. "It doesn't appear to be damaged; it looks the same as when you brought it to me."

Before Paisley could respond, Leo reached out and put the necklace around her neck.

36

Chapter Thirty-Six

"He did it, Mum! Before I could think of stopping him, he put the necklace around my neck!"

"And...nothing?"

"I felt a little warmth, that's all. Just for a moment, when he first put it on. That was it."

"So, why do you suppose nothing happened?"

"I thought about it on the way home, and I'm guessing that there are several factors that have to come into play. We talked about them, remember? First, it was on me, but nothing much happened. I think I'm part of the equation, but there must be more. Second, there was no stone. Then I wondered, does it have to be an emerald? Last, I wasn't at Thornberry Manor." Paisley stabbed at the scrambled eggs on her plate and ate a mouthful before continuing. "I'm wondering if all three things need to be in place, like the aligning of some mystical force or the planets in the solar system: Me, the necklace with a gemstone, and Thornberry Manor."

"Nothing is certain, now that the emerald is gone." Molly sipped her tea and took a bite of toast. "Do you have the necklace with you now?"

"No, I left it with Leo, because I should probably put something in the hollow where the emerald was." She smiled fondly at the mention of his name. "He's so worried about the necklace going missing again that he's going to keep it in their safe when he's not working on it." She finished her tea, cleared her place from the table, and hugged her still-seated mum from behind. "If he only knew, right?"

"It may never happen again. That's a possibility, too."

"You're right, Mum. You're absolutely right." Paisley picked up her phone and looked at the time. "I need to get dressed—it'll be time to open soon."

Half an hour later, Paisley followed her mum down the stairs into the shop. "One more thing about the necklace, then I'll give it a rest."

"What's that?"

"I would like to keep it—aside from everything else, it's a beautiful piece of jewellery. Leo can finish cleaning it and doing whatever else it needs; that will give me some time to come up with the money for something to replace the emerald."

"With what?"

"I don't know. I'll have to see what choices I can afford, but probably not an emerald." She moved down the aisle and straightened some books on the display tables. "Oh, I stopped at Greville Street Books and got some ideas for our next window displays. She raised the window shade, flipped the *Closed* sign to *Open*, and opened the door to catch a whiff of the warm, salty air.

Two groups of walkers paused in front of the shop as Paisley opened the door. "Are you open?" one woman asked.

"Good morning. We are, just now. Feel free to have a look around if you like." While the walkers browsed, Paisley swept the sidewalk in front of the door and tended the red geraniums in the large, clay pots on either side. Saturdays were good traffic days, full of promise for interesting conversations about books, authors, and subsequent decisions to purchase.

During a lull, Paisley checked the website, did a quick inventory of the books on hand for the summer promotion, and placed an order for what they'd need to have on hand. "People seem to like our magnets and bookmarks."

"They do. The bookmarks are free, and the magnets are an inexpensive souvenir that advertises our shop. Did you order more?"

"I did, Mum. Should be here sometime next week." Paisley scrolled through the online order. "Anything else before I submit?"

"I don't think so. I already did the candles and small gift items. I was going to look through the mysteries, but that's probably more of a fall thing. I'll try to get to it next week. In the meantime, I'll move some of these gardening books to a better location; people seem to be interested in them this time of year."

Paisley's phone pinged with a photo from Finlay. He was standing outside, his back to one of the walls of Thornberry; clinging to the stone behind him was a mass of rosebuds and some open, pink roses. She hurried over to her mum and showed her the photo. "Look, Mum, they're going to bloom!"

"Oh, they're beautiful! I can almost smell them."

Paisley smiled as she typed a quick answer.

Thank you for sending this! I hope I get to see them before they're done blooming.

She watched the sequential dots that told her Finlay was typing.

Will save one for you. Conservatory panels going in today – Frank, Scott, and a few extras on hand to get the job done. Ladders and some sort of crane/hoist on hand. Will send photos.

A wave of guilt flowed over Paisley. *I should be there, helping.*

Wish I could be there. Please be careful. You and the others. Photos...thanks! Will need them to include with my reports.

More sequential dots. The shop was filling with the musical chatter of book lovers, and her mum looked around to see where she was—she'd have to read his text later. She typed a quick message and set the phone aside as the bell above the door jangled once again.

Catch you later – busy day in the shop. XO

37

Chapter Thirty-Seven

"I know you'll have a long list when you visit Thornberry next, but when you have a break, can you look at these portraits and see if there are any names or identification of any kind on them? Front or back? I took these on my last trip up there, but didn't have a chance to take them down and inspect them." Molly looked on as Paisley took her phone and scrolled through the photos. "I'd like to be able to pair them up with my ancestry information."

"Sure, Mum. I'll see if I can find anything. Send them

to me in an email, and I'll reply with anything I find for each one." She stopped at one image from the drawing room. "This man looks familiar. I think it might be Flemon Hix."

"How do you know?"

Paisley smiled at her mum and whispered, even though there was no one else in the living room. "I met him, remember? He's Henry's father."

Molly gasped, then giggled. "Sometimes I forget that you were really there. What year was it again?"

"1829."

"Yes, the year Henry was born. I have the dates from his stone."

"Don't show them to me. We covered his stone at Thornberry, remember?"

"I do, but I still don't understand your aversion to seeing it."

"I don't understand it, either, but a voice from somewhere doesn't want me to know for some reason. For now, I have to go along with it. Maybe it will make sense later."

Paisley showed Molly the photo Finlay sent of the glass panels resting in the framework of the conservatory ceiling. "Isn't it beautiful? I can't wait to see it in person." She leaned back into the couch with a frustrated sigh. "You're sure Alice can't fill in so you can come with me?"

"I wish I could, but she's come down with the flu. She needs to be home in bed and away from here so she doesn't unintentionally infect me or any customers." Molly looked out the window over the choppy water. "It's so different there—like a completely different world."

"In more ways than one," Paisley added.

"When are you leaving?"

"Well, I could leave tomorrow, since the shop is closed on Sunday. That will make things easier for you. I could spend a few days, then be back before the busy weekend again. Will you be okay on your own?"

"I think that will work. If there's any downtime, I can inventory the mysteries and see what we might need for fall." Molly's tawny eyes looked tired, and Paisley couldn't help but feel guilty for leaving her to mind the shop alone.

"I'm sorry, Mum. I'll try to get back as soon as I can and help you." As Molly tightened the binder on her hair, Paisley noticed the glimmer of the grey strands amongst the brown. *It's getting to be too much for her.* She tried to think of something positive to turn things around. "Do you have any fabric that will work for sand in the windows? If you can find some, I'll set them up when I get back. If you don't have any fabric, I'll see if there's a store in Keighley where I can get some. I'm sure Finlay will give me a ride there and back—or from there to the train station on my way home."

"Okay. I'll look around and let you know." Molly got up and extended her hand to Paisley. "Let's go and sit in the garden, okay? It's out of the wind there, and we can see how things are coming along."

The tomato plants were blooming, and the rosemary left its signature scent on Paisley's hand when she brushed it against the stems. Orderly rows of carrot and radish tops sent a promise of a good harvest while the beans climbed toward the sky, clinging to bamboo stakes. "It all looks good, Mum."

Paisley followed her as they made their way slowly up and down the rows of the garden plot, discussing the progress, timelines, and next steps for the various plants in the efficient garden space.

They sat on the weathered, grey bench, separately and together savoring the moments of silence and the peaceful slowing of pace that surrounding oneself amongst growing things encourages. It was quiet and calm, with the sturdy, stone building sheltering them from any mischief churned up by the channel on the other side.

With her face to the sky and her eyes closed, Molly finally spoke. "Other than the portraits, what will you work on at Thornberry?"

Paisley remained in the same position as her mother. "Oh, there's always so much to do. I'll take more photos to send to the Historic England Board of the conservatory and anything else that's been completed since the last report I sent. If the conservatory roof is done, there will probably be a lot of cleaning and arranging I can do. I'd like to do that before I take photos for the board. I could probably spend my entire time just there, but I'll see what else needs my attention." She hoped her mum's eyes were still closed so she didn't see her smile at the thought of seeing Finlay again. "Is there anything other than the portraits that you had in mind?"

"Not really. Unless you have a chance to go back into the attic. We didn't get too far when we were up there."

"Maybe I should save that for the next trip you make with me—it'd be more fun with you there." Paisley glanced over at her mum and saw her smile.

"That's an idea. It will give me something to look forward to."

"On that note, I guess I should pack a few things and get ready for tomorrow."

They both got up and walked toward the kitchen door. Paisley opened the door for her mum, then followed her in. "Any ideas for supper tonight, or should we order something for delivery?"

"Fish and chips?"

"Yeah, that'll do just fine. I'll order, Mum. Why

don't you have a nice soak in the tub? By the time you're out, it should be here."

After she placed the order, she called Finlay. He answered on the third ring. "Hi, Sweet."

"Hi, Handsome. Thought I'd take the chance at actually talking to you instead of texting."

"You're timing is perfect. I just dropped off some clients and I'm on my way back to the inn. What's up?"

"I'm coming to Thornberry tomorrow. Any chance you'll be able to pick me up at the train station around four?"

"Oh, about a 100% chance, I'd say."

"I ordered some groceries for delivery Monday, but I won't want to cook tomorrow after travelling all day. Can you bring us something from the inn and put it on my card?"

"Sure. What would you like?"

"Anything except fish and chips—we're having that tonight."

"I'll figure something out, along with something sinful for dessert."

"I was hoping you'd be the sinful part."

"Oh, I am, and I will be. Trust me, I have it well in hand."

"You? That's my job, Finlay Wood."

"Hold that thought, Paisley Venne."

38

Chapter Thirty-Eight

Paisley was tired and pleasantly, suitably sore when she kissed Finlay goodbye in the still-dark hours of Monday morning. He had visitors to pick up at the train station and deliver to the Silent Inn, then do what he could with the ever-present maintenance list Olivia had waiting for him.

When the morning sky brightened, she ventured into the conservatory to see the restored ceiling. Murmuring with pleasure and amazement at the transformation, she wandered aimlessly in the space, admiring the impressive job Finlay and the others had done. The room radiated with a soft, warm glow that would brighten as the sun climbed higher in the sky. "This will do nicely," she announced to the plants, random pieces of furniture, and the orange tree posted outside the door. After taking a few photos to send to the Board, she went inside to start on the portrait project.

Those hanging on either side of the fireplace were definitely Flemon Hix and his wife Polly, but Paisley took them down to inspect them and see if there was anything written on the back. She sent photos of them to her mum, along with their dates for confirmation.

Hi, Mum! Starting portrait project. I'll send these to you as I come across them and can ID. First two from drawing room — either side of fireplace:

Flemon Hix: 1804-1856. Polly Hix: 1809-1858. Dates from stones in cemetery.

Those were the easy ones—she recognized them because she'd met them in person. In 1829. She laughed out loud and shook her head in disbelief as she returned them to their places on the wall. They'd need a good cleaning; she'd ask Finlay if he knew anyone. Otherwise, she'd have to take them to London. If it came to that, she'd ask Leo. Maybe he could recommend someone.

"Okay, on to the next." On another wall of the drawing room was a landscape that looked like a view of the lake and surrounding lawn and forest. "Portraits. Just portraits for now." In a small niche, Paisley found a smaller portrait that drew her to it. Two children, a girl and a boy, were seated on a bench under a tree with the lake in the background. The young girl looked at the viewer, while the smaller boy appeared to be watching something off in the distance. The artist had delicately and somewhat discretely added the small, comma-shaped birthmark under his left ear. Paisley's breath caught in her throat. Could it be him? Young Henry? The baby she'd held in her arms?

She gently lifted the painting from the wall and studied the two, young subjects as the sound of precocious Phoebe's laughter and infant Henry's cries seemed to echo in the room. The identity of the artist remained unknown, but it was the subjects Paisley was most interested in, anyway. She found their names and the year written on the back of the portrait. *1836. Phoebe and Henry Hix.*

She took a photo of the front and back of the portrait and sent it to her mum.

These are Flemon and Polly's children—Phoebe and Henry. Phoebe: 1827-1847. Henry: born 1829, and please do not tell me his death date. For some reason, I'm not supposed to, or can't, know. You can add to your database without telling me.

It was a relief to step away from Henry and his immediate family. Paisley moved into the study and found an older portrait of a couple, whose names were Cornelius and Pearl Hix. Based on the 1700s date, she remembered them as Flemon's parents, and he was the man who'd built Thornberry Manor. Photo and text sent. Her mum could sort that one out. The remaining paintings didn't have any people in them, but Paisley found an old photograph in the drawer of a side table. She gently slid what looked like a wedding photo out of its frame, turned it over, and hoped someone had identified it. Luck was on her side.

The couple, married on January 5th of 1977, were probably the last people to live in Thornberry Manor. They were identified on the back of the photo as John B. Hicks and his wife Margaret. She left it out of the frame and leaned it up against a vase to eliminate any glare.

Interesting, how the spelling of the last name changed. I wonder when that happened. John B. and Margaret Hicks. Probably the last relative to live here before you inherited. Pretty sure you have his dates from the cemetery—his is the newest-looking stone. And Rachel's is next to theirs. Let me know if you need photos of their stones, but I think we got them all the last time we were up there.

There were no portraits in the dining room, and the last, logical place was the attic. She thought about going up there, but it would be more fun with her mum. Besides, the sun and clear skies were beckoning, and she wanted to see the blooming roses.

Their sweet, heavy scent filled the space outside the conservatory; it swirled on the breeze, wafting around her before she saw the mass of petals clinging to the stone. Her careful pruning had encouraged them to flourish, branch out, and climb higher. With any luck, they'd be on their way to the roof next summer.

As she turned the corner and walked toward the main entrance, a bit of brass on the stone wall at the foot of the stairs caught her eye. The foliage against the wall hid it from a straight-on view, but from where Paisley was, the brass against the stone warranted immediate investigation. "Oh my gosh," Paisley whispered as she moved the branches away for a clear view. It was a commemoration plaque, from when Thornberry Manor was built. She proudly read it aloud.

Thornberry Manor
Built on this site in 1750
By
Cornelius I. Hix

Paisley ran back into the conservatory for a set of pruners and carefully removed any greenery that blocked the plaque. "A little brass polish will have it looking proud again." She took a photo of it and sent it to her mum.

From the front of the house. Plants were covering it, and I just happened to find it. File in your database under Cornelius I. Hix—this is a great find!

Paisley XO

The section of the kitchen garden that had been unearthed was beginning to show off its wares. The mint was abundant, and Paisley hoped that the rhubarb at the far end that had gone wild could be tamed and harvested again. Mum would know about that. She thought about pulling weeds to see what else had promise, but that was a task she knew her mum would enjoy and that they could do together. That, and the attic. She'd save those for the two of them.

The breeze accompanied her up the steps and through the gate to the cemetery. Her heart felt an urgency to visit the graves of the portrait faces she'd seen inside. She stopped at Cornelius' grave and silently thanked him for building Thornberry. Flemon and his family were nearby, with Henry's side still wrapped in its cardboard warning; Paisley paused but moved on to the stone of John B. Hicks and his family. "I'm sorry you're gone, but your passing has made it possible for Mum and I to carry on as best we can."

She sat against the warm, stone wall in the sunshine and listened to the fluttering leaves, birdsong, and the buzzing of bees visiting the wildflowers scattered among the gravestones. There was so much life surrounding the dead, and Paisley felt a peaceful feeling of acceptance to be in the company of her ancestors. Some people might have found it odd or unnatural to find comfort in a cemetery, but Paisley wasn't among strangers. They were her family. She embraced their memory, thanking them for all they had done to make it possible for her to be alive, soaking up the sun and sitting with them.

She wasn't sure how long she'd dozed off but woke in the cooling shade to the sound of Finlay calling her name.

39

Chapter Thirty-Nine

"What are you doing here, hanging out with the dead?" Finlay strode through the gate with a concerned look on his face and pulled her into his arms. "I couldn't find you in the house; I was afraid something had happened to you."

"I'm fine, Finlay—even better now that you're here." She gave him a kiss, then turned back to the scattered, mis-matched stones and markers of her ancestors. "I was working inside, identifying some portraits for Mum. Then I decided to come out here and spend some time with them. I guess I fell asleep."

Finlay took her hand and led her through the gate, closing it behind them. "Come away, now. Leave the dead to their rest and return to the world of the living."

They went in through the conservatory where Paisley stopped Finlay under the dome. "I can't believe how beautiful it is. You and your workers did an amazing job; it's like you turned back time." She circled slowly with her face tilted to the source of the soft light flooding the space around them. "I love that we were able to re-create the original panels." She walked around the space with Finlay's hand in hers. "This will be beautiful once we get it cleaned up and new furniture added. Visitors will love spending time here. For now, it's good to have it enclosed to the weather."

Finlay stepped back and closed the conservatory door. "We might get some rain overnight. The orange tree looks happy, but no fruit this year. That's okay, though. It takes a lot of energy to recover from neglect. Maybe next year, fingers crossed."

"We'll have to bring it in for the winter. I don't want to risk losing it to a freeze."

"We won't forget, and it's only June—there's still plenty of time for it to enjoy its time outdoors."

Paisley led Finlay into the study. She stood in front of the bookshelves, purposely ignoring what she felt was the most important book in the entire collection. "Maybe doors for the bookshelves will be a good fall/winter project. I'm anxious to get them covered and protected."

"It's never too early to get the materials ordered. I can take some measurements tomorrow and have them framed up for glass inserts."

"And locks. We need to be able to lock them." Paisley gently ran her fingers along the spines of a series of leather-bound books. "When you're ready, I'll take them out, so you have room to work without worrying about damaging them. I haven't really had a chance to see what's here, so it will be a fun project. For me, anyway. I love books."

"The dining room is the one I think will be spared from the most disruption. Aside from any electrical issues, it can stay the way it is. And the dumb waiter will be a godsend." Paisley took a seat in one of the dark, claw-footed chairs. "We could eat dinner in here tonight, except I haven't done a thing about it."

"Well, how about going down to the kitchen and see what we have to work with?"

Paisley smiled up at him. "I see something I'd like to work with, right here."

"Right here? Right now?" With a wicked, seductive smile, Finlay reached out and lifted her onto the smooth, dark tabletop. His voice was low and husky, barely above a whisper. "You won't hear any argument from me."

263

Clothes and undergarments hurriedly and haphazardly littered the floor, Finlay took a breath between kisses in order to pull Paisley to the edge of the table, and made an announcement as he quickly and passionately thrust into her. "I think we should dedicate every room at Thornberry this way. I'm willing to bet that we're the first to use the table for something other than dining. Or should I say, the partaking of food?"

"Oh, Mr. Brown. That's quite scandalous of you." Paisley laughed as her hands explored every bit of him that she could reach.

Finlay covered her with kisses as the table rhythmically creaked to their lovemaking. "Well, Ms. Venne, I'm not doing this alone, am I?"

Paisley did her best to catch her breath. "This table, this room will never be the same."

"Nor will any of the other rooms when we're done with them. Just you wait."

At the end, Finlay slowly withdrew and sank back into the chair at the head of the table while Paisley lay splayed on its surface in front of him. When she moved, a slippery, squeaky sound made her laugh. "I think we've added a new finish to the surface of this table."

"I daresay we have." She slid off with another squeak and pulled on Finlay's shirt. "I'm just going to borrow this until I go upstairs and find something else to wear."

Finlay pulled on his jeans and socks. "In the meantime, I'll go downstairs and see if there's anything there that we can put together for dinner. I don't know about you, but I'm starved."

"Maybe you can be as inventive in the kitchen as you were just now."

"I'm not sure how that translates, but I'll give it a shot."

Twenty minutes later, they were back in the dining room with omelets, toast, and candles. "I've never actually eaten a meal in this room," Paisley said as she looked around, then at Finlay.

"I have."

"When?"

"About an hour ago."

Paisley blushed. "You were a bit tenacious, if I say so myself." She leaned back in the chair and extended her arms to take in the tabletop scene. "It's like in the movies, you know?"

"What?"

"The couple has sex, then eats eggs by candlelight. We're not in the kitchen, but close enough, right?"

Finlay smiled as he jabbed and chased the last bites of egg on his plate. "Whatever you say, Love." He set his fork down and kissed her. "No matter the film, I think we have it beat." Paisley smiled with amusement as he took hold of the edge of the table and gently rocked it back and forth. "Need to be sure we didn't weaken any joints." He wiped his hands on his napkin and pushed his plate away. "Now, how about filling me in on this portrait project? I'm assuming that's what led you to the cemetery."

Paisley felt a slice of tension creep in, but was pretty sure she could explain everything away. "When Mum inherited Thornberry, she decided to subscribe to one of those ancestry sites and find out about our family history. We looked at some of the portraits in the house, and she wanted me to see if I could find any names on them to match them up with what she's got in her tree."

"Any luck?"

"Yes, as a matter of fact. A couple of them in the drawing room are people who lived in the 1800s. Oh, and I was meaning to ask you—do you know of anyone in the area who cleans paintings? If not, I'll ask Leo at the jewellery store in London when I go there next."

"Why are you going back? I thought your necklace was lost in the robbery."

"Oh, I forgot to tell you! I went there to pay him for the work he'd done before it was lost. When I was getting ready to pay him, my debit card fell between the display cases, and when we were fishing it out, we found a few rings … and my necklace."

"Do you have it with you?"

"No, I left it with Leo because I need to replace a stone that was damaged, and I haven't figured out what it will be."

"Damaged? How did it get damaged?"

Paisley was determined not to lie, but she had a find a way to tell Finlay without telling him. "I'm not exactly sure, but the stone just sort of crumbled, and I want to replace it with something. I'm not sure what it will be. I'm hoping Leo can help me with that."

"It doesn't sound like an ordinary piece of jewellery. Why is this one so special?"

Paisley toyed with the corner of her napkin, then started gathering up the dishes. "Actually, I found it here in the house. I'm not sure how old it is or who it belonged to, but I want to keep it. It may have ties to someone in my family." She'd already said more than she meant to, so she took Finlay's empty plate and gave him a kiss. "Now, we should try to get some actual sleep since Scott and Frank will be here in the morning."

Finlay groaned. "So, no sleeping in or easing into the morning if you know what I mean."

"Yes, I do, and if you mean what I think you do,

there won't be time for anything lengthy or prolonged."

Finlay laughed as he climbed the stairs next to her. "If I get some rest, I won't need anything lengthy or prolonged—just like tonight." At the top, he laughed softly as he put his arm around her. "C'mon, Sweet. First things first. Set your alarm if you must, then let's get some sleep. I may talk like some macho, sex machine, but I'm just a tired, gratefully satisfied man who needs rest."

40

Chapter Forty

"The bathrooms should be ready for fixtures by day's end," Frank said as he tightened the connection on the shutoff valve. "I can start on the kitchen whenever you're ready, but that might involve some days where the water is shut off." Frank Blackburn was easy-going, dependable, and didn't mince words. Paisley appreciated his forthcoming nature, and the fact that he was a bit older lent credibility to his knowledge of his trade and the reputation he'd built up over the years.

She waited for him to straighten up, then smiled at his workworn face and green eyes. He was old enough to be her father, and she respected him for the hard work he was probably forced to do under less-than-ideal circumstances. New construction was probably something for him to look forward to, although the kitchen might prove to be something of a challenge. Still, she noticed that he moved with a bit of a painful stoop, probably the result of having to crawl and twist into spaces not kind to the human body. She hoped he'd be able to retire soon, stretch his aching, contorted limbs, and sleep until noon if he wanted to.

"I hope the kitchen doesn't cause you too much trouble," Paisley said as she handed him a wrench that was just out of his reach. *I need him to finish Thornberry before he retires.*

"Oh, I think it will come along nicely. It's a pretty basic room that just needs some upgrades to conform to present-day codes. If you're not making any major changes, it will be fine."

"We will need a dishwasher, and the laundry area will need proper plumbing. New appliances, but in the same location."

"Yes, you've got that in your plan, and we'll make sure the drain pipes inside and out are running free and clear."

Paisley hesitated to ask, sensing Frank's pride and dedication, but she needed to know that Frank was being compensated for his work. "The payments from the Board, they're coming through okay? On time, and correct?"

"They're coming through just fine—smooth as silk." Frank didn't smile often; he was always polite, but focused on his business and the job at hand. When he did, the dimples in his cheeks warmed her heart. They reminded her of her dad.

"Good. I'm glad to hear it. I'm sending them regular updates, reports, and photos, and I need to be sure they're holding up their end of the bargain." She followed him down the stairs to the kitchen. "I'm here until Friday, but there's plenty to do around here that doesn't involve water."

Frank left after reviewing the upgrades for the kitchen, and Paisley hurried back upstairs to catch Scott and make sure his payments were coming through as well. "Just fine, Paisley," he said as he snipped three wires and twisted on a wire nut. "We'll be ready for fixtures soon. We can look at what you have and see if you want to keep them. If you do, I can re-wire them for you."

"That would be awesome. If you can take down the existing ones, I'll clean them up and you can let me know what's worth keeping."

Paisley and Scott agreed that he would look at any

fixtures Paisley wanted to save on his next trip out. "I should probably paint the ceilings before we put them up." Paisley looked around, thinking about where to purchase paint. Finlay would know, so would Scott. White or eggshell for the ceilings, then she could think about colors for the rooms. As she walked with Scott to his truck, she asked him about local paint suppliers.

After Scott left, she made a sandwich and found a sunny spot in the partially-unearthed kitchen garden. In between bites, she researched and made notes of the names of various roses and their colors for each room: Benjamin Britten (deep red), Molineux (golden yellow), Mary Rose (soft pink), Heritage (pinkish/peach), and Abraham Darby (pale apricot). It would be fun to give them a name and color based on England's beautiful roses. The walls would be pale and muted, or maybe even a neutral ivory, but it would be a creative and fun way to identify them and give each one its own personality. She conjured up images of pretty plaques on each door with the names on them.

Her mum might know of some other varieties or have a completely different idea, so she sent her the list in a text to see what she thought. They could always change to a variety of native flowers, like bluebell, daisy, or buttercup. As she finished the text, the sounds at Thornberry prompted her to set down her phone, close her eyes, and immerse herself in the impromptu concert in the late-afternoon sun. Soft breezes, chipper birdsong, and the buzzing of bees and other insects floated on the balmy air in an ever-changing, soothing, and restful melody—one that had probably played out in various forms at the manor house for hundreds of years.

The sound of Finlay calling her name jolted her from her dream-like state and prompted her to jump up and wave. "Back here, Finlay."

He greeted her with a smile, a kiss, and a strong, wrap-around hug. "Hi, Sweet," he whispered in her ear.

"Hi, Fin," she said with a smile. "Do you mind the shortened version? I'm trying to find an affectionate name to call you. "Honey sounds so cliché, and you call me Sweet. Any suggestions?"

Finlay grinned and took her hand. "How about a walk along the lake? Maybe something will present itself."

They started off in the sun-drenched lawn directly in front of the manor, then followed the tree-shaded spaces along the western shore. "I wonder sometimes..." Paisley started, "about the people who lived here. My ancestors. I wonder about their lives—were they good people?" She looked around, extending her arm in the direction they were headed. "Did any of them walk where we are now? Who were they, and what did they talk about? Did they think about what life would be like for future generations?"

She felt dangerously close to telling Finlay about the necklace and visiting Thornberry in 1829, but something pulled her back. The warning came again, soft and insistent: *Keep it secret. Keep it safe.* She'd already told her mum; that was more than she'd planned to do, but at the time she felt if she didn't tell someone, she'd go mad.

Finlay's voice interrupted her thoughts. "Well, you and your mum are researching your history and your ancestors who lived here. Maybe that will shed some light on the kind of people they were." He paused for a moment, then stopped and faced her. "I could take you to the church in Keighley and see what kinds of records they have. You have birth and death records from the ancestry site, but there may be other documents that might tell you something about them." He paused again, doing what looked like some sort of calculation in his mind. "I'm booked solid tomorrow, but how about Thursday? I can take you over in the morning, run a couple of errands, and pick you up when you're done."

"Oh, my gosh! I hadn't thought about local records. I'd love to do some research. Do you know what church might have them? I'm assuming there's more than one church in Keighley."

"I'm pretty sure it would be St. Andrews, but I'll

check with them to be sure."

"Maybe I have to make an appointment with someone, or at least let them know I'm coming to look at records."

"I can call now; someone might still be there." Finlay took her hand and turned her back toward the house. "Time to return to the present. I'll make that call, and you can see if there's anything to put together for dinner. Deal?"

"Deal."

"And." He stopped mid-sentence to deliver a warm, prolonged kiss. "Tonight, you are mine. All mine." He grinned and kissed her again. "And don't count on getting much sleep."

Paisley laughed and ran toward the house ahead of him. "Okay, I won't."

41

Chapter Forty-One

Thursday dawned in a shroud of mist and fog. Paisley was glad for it; she'd spent all of Wednesday raking the beds of the climbing roses next to the walls, then feeding and watering them. Spent petals fluttered like pale, cupped snow to the ground while new blooms clung to the stony façade, dispatching their scent on the warm, gentle breeze.

Paisley stood next to the low, stone wall at the edge of the driveway, waiting for Finlay to collect her. She took a couple of steps and assessed the wall; it was nearly covered in ivy that would need a severe trimming or outright removal. Thoughts about options or replacements were put on hold as Finlay's truck turned onto the gravel drive. She took a quick photo and decided to ask her mum when she returned home.

She smiled as Finlay pulled to a stop, then climbed inside.

"Hi, Sweet." He gave her a kiss and squeezed her hand. "Got everything you need?"

Paisley patted her bag and nodded. "Phone with details, notebook, and pen. Not sure what else I need." She rested her hand on his leg as he turned out of the driveway and onto the narrow, paved road leading to Keighley. "Who is it I'm meeting with? I've forgotten her name."

"Mrs. Forster. First name is Gracie. Sweet as can be, and I'm sure she'll be happy to help you find whatever they might have in the church records."

"I'm not sure how long I'll be. Could be ten minutes or most of the day."

"Don't worry. I have a flexible schedule today, so I can swing by and deliver you back to the manor when you're done unless there's something else you want to do."

"Well, I was thinking about ceiling paint, starting in the upstairs rooms; that's the next step in the process. I could buy it, and it would be there, ready to go on my next trip up. Do you know where I can get some?"

"Right there," Finlay pointed as they passed. "We can stop after your appointment with Mrs. Forster." He turned the truck onto North Street and made the climb to the top.

"Oh, what a lovely church," Paisley said, admiring the stone building with its Gothic-arched windows and clock tower. "I can't wait to see the inside."

"There's Mrs. Forster, waiting for you." Finlay jumped out and opened the door for Paisley, then made the introductions. "Send me a text when you're done, and I'll come and collect you." He gave Paisley a gentle squeeze on the arm and thanked Mrs. Forster before climbing back into his truck and returning down the hill, giving her a wave and thumbs-up out the open window.

"I've got tea and biscuits inside, then we can get started," Mrs. Forster said with a warm, welcoming smile. She was short and sturdy with grey eyes that sparkled when she smiled. She fussed with her salt-and-pepper curls as she climbed the steps, then pulled the solid, oak door open for them. "And please, call me Gracie."

"I guess my official title is Office Secretary," she explained as they walked up the main aisle of the church. Paisley looked back and forth over the pews at the stories in the stained-glass windows, dark wood, and listened to the sound of her steps on the stone pavers under her feet. In a small room off the main part of the church, Gracie invited Paisley to sit at a small, oak table. She poured tea for both of them and extended the plate of biscuits to Paisley.

"Thank you," Paisley said, taking a grateful sip of the steaming breakfast blend with cream and sugar.

"You can probably guess that my position involves much more than correspondence. I don't mind, really. The variety keeps things interesting, especially helping people with their family histories. There seems to be a lot more of that these days."

As she gathered up the remnants of their tea break, she pointed to a door at one end of the room. "We'll work in there on your records search."

The long, oak table held several large, old books bound in faded, aged leather. Paisley pulled out her notebook and pen as Gracie handed her a pair of white, cotton gloves. "We can start with the oldest records and work our way forward." She carefully opened the book to the marker she'd inserted. "Here is the first mention of your ancestors that I found. It's a census of sorts and lists Cornelius Hix and his wife Pearl. They built Thornberry Manor in 1750."

Paisley already knew that from their prior research but remained silent and nodded, hoping for more as Gracie turned the page. "There isn't much to note for his son

William and wife Prudence except for their birth and death certificates and donations to the church. Perhaps they had a relatively uneventful life."

Gracie turned to the next marker. "Then we have their son Flemon and wife Polly. These are the baptismal records for their children, Phoebe and Henry. Phoebe, born in 1827, and Henry two years later, in 1829."

"Do you mind if I take a photo of them with my phone?"

"No, of course not." Gracie carefully held the pages for Paisley before moving to the next marker. "These are the birth and death certificates for Primrose, Phoebe's daughter. And, sadly, here is Phoebe's. Based on the dates, we can assume she died in childbirth, and the baby died as well."

"Such a sad turn of events," Paisley whispered. "Is there any information about the father of the baby?"

"We don't have a marriage certificate for her, but it's possible that she wasn't married in this church, or any church. A service could have been conducted in the home, for instance."

"But her name on the death certificate is listed as Phoebe Hix, so wouldn't that mean that she never married?"

"I suppose so. Or, the marriage was never recorded here. We may never know about that."

Tears stung at Paisley's eyes at the memory of

meeting the vibrant, blonde-haired little girl. Of course, she was no longer alive; nearly two hundred years had passed. But Paisley couldn't help thinking about the documentation of this sad, tragic event and wondered if there had been any happy moments in Phoebe's life.

Gracie whispered in a sympathetic, stoic voice as she closed the book. "Let's move on, shall we?" She slid the next book in front of them. "There is information in here on Henry and his parents."

Paisley took a photo of Henry's birth certificate, then closed her eyes as she took one of his death certificate. She waited, eyes squeezed shut, until she heard the turning of the brittle, fragile page. Was she ever going to learn the reason for her avoiding the knowledge of his death? It was beginning to border on the ridiculous. If she didn't know better, she'd rationalize that it was some sort of dream or fantasy and put it all behind her. Except it wasn't. It had really happened.

After documenting Flemon and Polly's certificates, Gracie called her attention to an unusual document. "I'm assuming this was done through the church in order to keep it confidential," she explained as she pointed out the regularly-scheduled entries. "It appears as though Flemon was paying for the care and upbringing of a child not in his immediate family. The payments were made to the mother listed as Annabelle Eaton, beginning in 1829. We'll learn a bit more about the child in the next book."

Paisley drew in a sharp breath as she remembered Annabelle coming to collect Phoebe and Henry on the day of her visit. Then she saw the payment entries for a wet nurse. "Does it say anything about how old Annabelle was?" Paisley remembered the quiet, dark-haired woman as being young, perhaps too young to be a mother. Her research had taught her that women married younger in earlier centuries, but the payment entries seemed to indicate they were being made quietly and no one was to know about them.

"No. No age is listed for Annabelle in this journal."

"And nothing about the identity of the father of Annabelle's baby?"

"No. Not directly. But the payments were made by Flemon Hix; his signature is at the end of every entry, authorizing it. So, there's that. And it appears that she continued working in the household for some years."

Paisley noted the dates of the first and last entries, and they moved on—she'd do the math later.

The last book Gracie showed Paisley revealed the name of Annabelle's daughter, Elizabeth Eaton. The previous book documented the payments starting in 1829, the same year Henry was born. In 1839, ten-year-old Lizzie was listed as a maid's helper, which would have been an appropriate role for her. Paisley couldn't help but wonder about Polly's reaction to the entire situation. Was Flemon Elizabeth's father? Or was he just being charitable to a young woman who found herself in trouble? There was no way to know for sure. Whatever the truth, perhaps Polly chose to remain ignorant to the unfolding drama around her or accepted it as something in life she had little/no control over.

Paisley remembered Polly as having a harsh, hardened side to her and wondered if events like these in her life had brought those feelings to the forefront. There was no way to know, but her opinion of Polly softened with the knowledge of the difficult burden she may have had to bear.

"Do you have any information on John B. Hicks? He was the last relative to live at Thornberry before we inherited it." Paisley scrolled through her phone for a photo of his grave marker. "His dates are 1945 to 2023—he died in September of '23. His wife's name was Margaret, who died in 2000, and they had a daughter, Rachel, who died in 1991."

"Those dates are fairly recent, so they'd be on the computer. Let's go into my office." Gracie pulled up a chair for Paisley next to hers and opened the database of the church's member history. It was efficiently organized by year, then alphabetically by name. "John officially joined the church in 1976, and he and Margaret were married here on January 5th, 1977." She opened up the attachments to the entry. "Do you want a copy of their birth and marriage certificates?"

"That would be great. I'm not sure we have those." Gracie clicked the print button, and the machine on the stand in front of the window whirred into action. "What about their funerals? Were they held here for any of them?"

Gracie clicked on another tab named *Funerals*. "Do you have death dates for any of them?"

"Yes, for all. John died in 2023, Margaret in 2000, and Rachel in 1991."

Gracie spoke as she scrolled. "You might want to check with the library for articles about them. They would be listed in the obituary section and might provide additional information about their lives."

"I hadn't thought of that. Thanks. The newspapers would be a great resource." Paisley quickly scribbled a note. "Would it be the local library here?"

"Yes, on North Street. Just a short distance from here. But if you're doing research, it's best to make an appointment. They're closed on Sunday and Monday, and alternate Saturdays." After a few clicks, Gracie landed at the entry for John. "No funeral for him here." A few more clicks, and she was finished. "None of them had a funeral service here. Not entirely unusual. The priest could have performed a small, simple service at the home before burial."

Paisley sighed with relief. A few more pieces had fallen into place. "I can't thank you enough for the time you've spent with me today. It means so much to fill in these details about my family."

"You're most welcome. It's part of my job, but it's gratifying to help others and make the occasional trip back in time."

"How much are the copies? I need to pay you for those."

Gracie sweetly scoffed. "There aren't enough to worry about. I'm happy to have been able to provide you with some information and answers." She walked Paisley to the door and opened it to a burst of sunshine. "Well, that's a pleasant surprise. I thought the clouds were going to be our constant companions today."

"It is looking good," Paisley said with an upturned face to the sky. "Thank you again, Gracie."

"You're welcome, Paisley. If other questions come up, feel free to call or stop by."

"I will. 'Bye now." With a wave, Paisley started down the hill toward the paint store she and Finlay had passed on the way to the church. Paisley pulled out her phone and sent a quick text.

Meet you at the paint store. I'll get started picking out
ceiling colors and then wait for you. XO

42

Chapter Forty-Two

"What do you think about my ideas for the bedrooms at Thornberry, Mum?" It was Sunday, the shop was closed, and Paisley and her mum were relaxing in their living room above the shop. "Did you like the idea of rose varieties for each room, or would you rather have something else?"

Molly took a sip of her iced tea before answering. "I do like the rose idea, but I think the various wildflowers that grow in the area will be more interesting; it will give each room more distinction, and visitors may see some of the actual, live flowers when they walk around the grounds." She pulled out a slip of paper and handed it to Paisley. "I jotted down a few ideas after you texted me."

Paisley looked at the list and smiled. "Actually, I like this better than all roses."

"We can keep the colors pale and muted, but I love the idea—violet, hawthorn, cowslip, and primrose. Pale shades of violet, rosy-pink, yellow, and blue. And the large bedroom, the one you and I have stayed in, could be whatever you want. Maybe ivy, a soft green. Or, a rose color that you like. Perhaps an ivory room with a deep, red accent or something like that."

"Oh, I love your idea, Mum. We can get cute signs to put on the doors, identifying each room. It will be so much fun, picking out linens and accent pieces." She shifted on the couch and glanced out the window at the water beyond the road. It was quiet today, with just a hint of movement. "It's so green and lovely up there just now—so different than here. You need to come up before summer is over, Mum."

"For certain. We need to finish up in the attic, look at the kitchen garden, and make lists for each room."

"I ordered ceiling paint when Finlay brought me into Keighley to meet with Gracie at the church. I'm hoping they can get the bedrooms done, then we can look at putting the fixtures back up. I want to use the original ones if we can, and Scott said he'd re-wire those that are worth saving."

"Perhaps another trip to the paint store to pick out wall colors for the rooms?"

"Absolutely!" Paisley set her bowl of crisps aside. "I've been thinking, Mum. At some point, I think I need to get a vehicle to use when I'm up there. I can't keep depending on Finlay to chauffer me around."

Molly's brow knit with concern. "Everything okay between you two?"

Paisley laughed. "Yes, Mum. Everything is fine with us."

"Good. Just needed to be sure. Perhaps he can look around up there for something suitable."

"It will probably have to be a small truck, with all that will be going on. A car just won't cut it." She typed a quick note in her phone. "Reminding myself to ask the Board about a vehicle. Maybe they can fund part of it or give me a decent interest rate since it will be directly connected to running Thornberry."

"Can't hurt to ask." Molly said after another sip of tea. "So, what's on your agenda for next week?"

"Well, I need to go to London and see Leo about the necklace."

"Ooh…the necklace."

"Yes, Mum, the necklace. I'm sure he's finished any cleaning and repair, and I need to choose another stone to fill the space where the emerald was."

"Any ideas of what you'll put there?"

"No. I'm hoping Leo can offer up something I can afford."

"And no one knows?"

"No one knows but us. You and me, Mum. Our secret, right?"

Molly scoffed. "Good gracious, Paisley. I can keep a secret—especially one like that."

"Just making sure. Anyway, I thought I'd go tomorrow and see what can be done about it. Then I'll help you work on the inventory here at the shop, and I suppose it will be time to change out the display windows again. Maybe grilling and picnic food books on one side and hiking/exploring Britain books on the other. I'll see what we have on hand and place an order if need be. Dig out my hiking boots, clean them up a bit, and put them in the window along with some walking sticks, a backpack, and a water bottle. Stuff like that. And maybe books about other people's travels."

"You always come up with the best ideas, Poppet."

"Thanks, Mum, but I sometimes steal bits and pieces of ideas from others." She looked out the window once more, admiring the golden, slanting sun settling itself against the surface of the water. "How about a walk before supper?"

The Farrington tube stop had begun to feel familiar as Paisley stepped off the train and turned in the direction of Bleeding Heart Yard on her way to Theodore & Son Jewellers. Leo had called her, telling her he'd cleaned and checked the necklace over. What it needed now was a new stone, something to fill the blank space left by the emerald. She'd left the crumbled bits with him on her first visit. Was there any point in keeping them? She wasn't sure, but decided she wanted the precious chips. After all, they were part of the original necklace, and whatever had happened would mostly likely not happen again, especially if the emerald was part of what she thought was the time-travel formula.

As she walked up the street, her 1829 visit to Thornberry Manor played like a movie in her head. Her mum had found the dress in the attic that she'd worn, and she'd met her ancestors Flemon, Polly, little Phoebe, and infant Henry. Their graves were in the cemetery, and she'd uncovered some of their history and learned something about their lives. Her avoidance of Henry's death date was still a mystery to her, but she allowed her intuition and instinct to guide her. She was sure at some point it would be revealed to her, along with the reason she wanted it withheld.

The chance, and memorable, meeting with Mary Shelley made her want to pinch herself as a reminder that it really happened. If she needed proof, it was right there on the bookshelf in the study—the copy of *Frankenstein* that she'd been gifted and that Mary had autographed for her. Paisley smiled to herself, pretending that she was enjoying the Monday sunshine as she walked along the street. It was something that defied explanation, and she was glad that her mum was the only other person that knew what had happened. Whatever or however, it wouldn't repeat itself now that the emerald was gone.

With a deep breath of air, she stepped inside Theodore & Son and greeted Leo.

"Ah! Good morning, Ms. Venne. It's a beautiful day to be out and about."

"It is, Leo." Paisley enjoyed seeing Leo; some of his mannerisms and his air of kindness reminded her of her father. And she had the feeling that he was adept at keeping confidences, should it become necessary. But today was reserved for choosing a stone to replace the damaged emerald. She hoped she'd be able to find a stone that would be a good fit for the setting, and something she could afford.

"I've cleaned it and checked the links and clasp," Leo said as he held it up for her to see. "Let's see how the length is when you have it on."

Before Paisley could object, Leo again placed the necklace over her head and settled it beside her neck. The chain was long enough to make the clasp unnecessary, but that wasn't what brought Paisley to a near panic. Would she disappear in front of Leo and end up somewhere in London, or somewhere else? In some other time? It hadn't happened the first time he did it, but she still wasn't sure how the necklace worked, if it even worked anymore. She was probably worrying about nothing.

"Are you quite well, Ms. Venne?"

Paisley opened her tightly-shut eyes just enough to see Leo looking at her with a look of genuine concern on his face. "Sorry. I was just imagining what it would feel like to wear it again."

Leo returned to the business at hand. "Well, the length looks appropriate, so I don't think we need to remove any links. That brings us to the final decision, to choose a stone to replace the emerald that was on the reverse side."

"Do you have the emerald bits, Leo? I've decided I'd like to keep them."

"I do, right here." He reached under the counter and gave Paisley the small, plastic container she'd brought with her the first time she'd brought him the necklace. She thanked him and slipped the container into her purse.

"Now, a replacement stone. Any recommendations?"

Leo pulled out the laminated sheet he'd shown her before. "Most of these are available; some will take longer than others to order. But here's something to consider." He smiled at Paisley, and his dark eyes sparkled. "We'll be running a promotion in July, the birthstone month for the ruby. I think that would be an excellent choice as a replacement."

"But it's not July yet..."

Leo leaned over the counter and winked. "I'll ensure you get the promotional price, nevertheless." He lifted out a small tray of rubies so Paisley could examine them and imagine one in the setting of her necklace. Every deep, red stone was beautiful, but Paisley was drawn to a smooth, oval cut gem that looked like it would be a perfect fit.

She pointed to it, then looked up at Leo with a smile. "I've made my choice, Leo. I choose a ruby."

Thank you!

Dear Reader,

I hope you enjoyed reading **Thornberry Manor: The Emerald**! Finding the inspiration for a story (in this case, the heart and soul of a series) is fascinating, intriguing, and most often where you least expect it. The idea for using a necklace came years after an impulse purchase one hot, summer day while on vacation in Savannah, Georgia.

The necklace seemed destined to be more than a piece of jewelry. One evening, the idea came to me, and the story was off and running! There was a lot more that had to be envisioned and created, but the necklace was the spark that set it all in motion. Who knew? I sure didn't!

If you have a few minutes, I'd love for you to post a review of **Thornberry Manor: The Emerald**. It doesn't have to be long and wordy and feedback is vital to a writer.

If you're so inclined, visit my website to see what's happening (the rest of the series) as well as what else is on the horizon: https://www.annehawkinson.com.

Thanks for reading **Thornberry Manor: The Emerald**!

ALSO BY ANNE K. HAWKINSON

(in chronological order)

Scotland's Knight: The Rose in the Glade (novella)
co-authored with Paul V. Hunter

Scotland's Knight: The Journey (novella)
co-authored with Paul V. Hunter

Scotland's Knight: The Hand of Fate (novella)
co-authored with Paul V. Hunter

Scotland's Knight: The Royal (novella)
co-authored with Paul V. Hunter

The Mystery at Moz Hollow (middle-grade novel)
written under the pen name A. K. Hicks

The Ghost Writer (novel)

Thornberry Manor: The Emerald (novel)

Thornberry Manor: The Ruby (novel)

ABOUT THE AUTHORS

Anne K. Hawkinson

AUTHOR

Anne was born in Duluth, Minnesota. The world's largest inland port became her "window to the world" when ships from around the globe crossed under the Aerial Bridge and docked in Lake Superior's harbor. Years later, she'd visit the countries that at one time existed only in her imagination.

Anne graduated from St. Cloud State University with a Master's degree in Special Studies (Art History, Creative Writing, and Photography), a Bachelor's degree in Art, and a Bachelor's degree in Art History.

Anne lives in the United States and writes for adults under the pen name of Anne K. Hawkinson and adventures for young readers under the pen name of A. K. Hicks.